'I don't know why you've come here, Silas . . .'

Even without looking at him she could feel his anger and she winced beneath the force of it.

'Let's forget the obligatory opening passages, shall we, Hannah? They aren't true, anyway. You know damn well why I've come here. The same reason I kissed you, the same reason you gave in your notice, the same reason you haven't got the guts to turn round and look at me now, damn you . . .'

And, without her knowing that he had moved, he was suddenly behind her, turning her round, holding her with such fierce urgency that her blood started to beat a wild tattoo of delirium through her veins, despite her attempts to stop it.

Books you will enjoy
by PENNY JORDAN

EQUAL OPPORTUNITIES

Kate Oakley desperately needed a nanny, otherwise she would never have dreamed of employing a man to look after nine-month-old Michael, her friend's orphaned baby. But Rick Evans had his own motives for wanting to be in her life . . .

A REASON FOR BEING

It was ten years since Maggie had naïvely hurt the man she worshipped, and now she had a chance to atone for her teenage wrongs by returning to help Marcus and his two half-sisters. She would, for as long as she had to—although it meant that she had to see her old love with his new fiancée . . .

VALENTINE'S NIGHT

Sorrel didn't particularly want to meet her distant cousin Val, but since the girl had come all the way from Australia it seemed churlish not to welcome her. But that was until she found herself snowbound in a remote Welsh hill farm with Val—who turned out to be very definitely male!

SO CLOSE AND NO CLOSER

After a disastrous marriage, Pue decided to opt for the solitary life, and was perfectly content—until Neil Saxton came along. He was demanding and dangerous—so why did she miss him when he wasn't around?

FREE SPIRIT

BY

PENNY JORDAN

MILLS & BOON LIMITED
ETON HOUSE 18-24 PARADISE ROAD
RICHMOND SURREY TW9 1SR

First published in Great Britain 1989
by Mills & Boon Limited

This edition 1989

ISBN 0 263 76447 8

Set in Palacio 10 on 11½ pt.
01–8910–51233

Typeset in Great Britain by JCL Graphics, Bristol

Made and Printed in Great Britain

CHAPTER ONE

'OH, YOU'RE off then, are you, darling?' Hannah's mother mourned, as Hannah came rushing into the kitchen, her weekend bag swinging from her shoulder.

It was a secret sorrow of Mrs Maitland's that, having produced four sons in succession before the arrival of a much longed for daughter, that daughter should turn out to be a determined career girl. She was proud of Hannah, of course she was, but she couldn't help feeling a little envious when her husband's parishioners mentioned family marriages and grandchildren.

With four sons scattered to the four corners of the earth, pursuing their chosen careers, surely it was only natural for her to wish that Hannah, her only daughter, had chosen to stay at home and settle down? Tom, her husband, laughed at her whenever she voiced this complaint, reminding her gently that Hannah had every right to choose her own way of living her life.

As she watched her crossing the kitchen, Rosemary Maitland studied her covertly. Even now, after twenty-six years, it still amazed her that she and Tom had produced this ravishingly beautiful creature, with her tall, slender body, and delicately oval-shaped face. Her tawny eyes had been inherited from Rosemary's own grandfather but, widely spaced and set between thick, dark lashes, Hannah's possessed an allure Rosemary could not remember her grandfather's having. Hair as tawny as her eyes, every conceivable shade of brown streaked with red and blonde, which nowadays was confined to a neat, elegant bob, had once curled half-way down her back until Hannah had announced that it was too untidy and not the image she wanted to project as a financial accountant.

Her daughter's choice of career was something that constantly amazed Rosemary. Where on earth had she got it from, this flair with figures? Certainly not from her, nor from Tom. Rosemary suppressed a small chuckle, remembering the many hours she and her husband had toiled over their household accounts.

A vicar's wife learned young how to manage on slender means, but they had been lucky; a generous bequest from a great-aunt had enabled them to educate all five children privately and to finance them through university.

'I'm sorry I've got to rush, Ma,' Hannah apologised, 'but I promised Linda that I'd call round. She's having problems with the Inland Revenue. She's got an appointment to see them this afternoon and I've promised I'll go with her. You know what she's like about figures. The mere sight of a column of them turns her into a dithering idiot, which is a shame because she's a marvellous businesswoman in every other sense.'

'Yes, I've heard that the shop's doing very well,' her mother agreed. 'I called in a few weeks ago and was dangerously tempted to buy the most beautiful tapestry cushion, Kaffe Fassett, I believe it was.'

Making a mental note to check with her friend on what exactly it was her mother had seen, Hannah went over to her and gave her a fond hug and a quick kiss. Her mother's birthday was coming up soon and the tapestry cushion would make a surprise present for her. Hannah had already bought her main present, a beautiful tweed suit from Jaeger, which she knew her mother would love.

'Give Linda my love, won't you?' her mother told her as she followed her out of the kitchen.

The vicarage was old and rambling and without the benefit of central heating, other than a very primitive handful of radiators that ran off the temperamental back boiler in the kitchen. Since this boiler required a fearsome amount of stoking to keep the radiators even moderately warm, it was the expressed opinion of the Maitland family that it was easier to do without the heating than to try to make it work. Her parents' life hadn't been an easy one, Hannah acknowledged, as she walked swiftly over to her car, and yet they were happy, far happier than the majority of her contemporaries' parents.

Her car had been a twenty-sixth birthday present to herself, a steel-grey Volvo, practical and sturdy.

'I'm sorry your father isn't here to see you off,' her mother apologised, as Hannah got into the driver's seat.

Hannah grinned, and for a moment it was possible for Rosemary Maitland to believe she was looking at Hannah as she had been as a teenager, all coltish legs and long, untidy hair. Now all that seemed to be left of that girl was that teasing grin, and even that was seldom in evidence these days. Hannah looked exactly what she was, a very successful businesswoman, dressed and groomed in a way that mirrored her lifestyle and her ambition, and looking at her, observing the elegant charcoal-grey pinstripe suit and the cream silk blouse designed like a shirt, without any feminine frills or flounces to it, Rosemary couldn't help feeling a little sad. She was proud of Hannah, of course she was, but she just wished that she would relax a little more; for instance, what had happened to that infamous temper Hannah had had as a child, a temper which her brothers had so often unkindly sparked off by tormenting her?

These days Hannah was everything that was reasoned and controlled. Too controlled, perhaps. Hannah started the engine and, with a final wave to her mother, set off down the overgrown drive.

The Dorset village which was home to her parents, and which had been home to her until she'd left for university, was small and picturesque, but that didn't mean that life for its inhabitants was without its problems. Parents mourned as their sons and daughters, unable to get jobs, moved away from home. Work on the land, which had once been labour-intensive, was now mechanised to such an extent that farm workers' cottages fell into disrepair as they became vacant, and farmers neither had the inclination nor the need to replace their workforce.

Now many of those cottages were being snapped up by people from London, up and coming career men and women, much like herself, with a keen eye for a bargain, and the knowledge that money invested in property was a wise investment. The village had changed even in her short lifetime.

Her father was close to retirement, and even though neither her father nor her mother had said anything Hannah knew they were both worrying about how they would manage and where they would live once her father had to give up the vicarage.

She and her brothers had discussed this problem the last time they were all together the previous Christmas. None of her brothers was married, preferring like her to be footloose and fancy free, and between the five of them they had agreed that they would all start saving towards being able to buy their parents a comfortable home.

After all, it was only right that they should do so, Mark had commented earnestly. Had their father invested his inheritance in bricks and mortar, instead of in their education, he would not be worrying about his retirement now.

Who else but a vicar would call his sons Matthew, Mark, Luke and John? Hannah wondered as she turned into the traffic. The boys took it well, even though there had been a period in their teens when all of them had opted to use their second and less conspicuous names. Once, their mother had confessed that it had been she who had called them after the Apostles, and Luke had teased her that the only reason she had chosen such names for them was because, in her disappointment at not producing the daughter she longed for so much, she had simply thought of the most convenient names.

Hannah had grown up surrounded by love and laughter. Her father was a gentle, intelligent man, who cared deeply about the human race and who suffered with it. Her mother was everything a vicar's wife should be: supportive, understanding, generous both with her time and her patience, cheerfully tolerant of the demands others made on her husband's time and of the financial hardship their life together had involved.

Even now, her mother still made her own jams and chutneys, still used every scrap of produce the huge, rambling vicarage garden gave, not so much these days because they needed it—after all, there were now only two mouths to feed, three if one counted Simon, a cat who had adopted them—but simply because for so many years she had not been able to afford to waste anything that now the habit had become ingrained with her. Hannah thought wryly of the half-opened cartons of this and that, discarded from her own fridge without a second thought. She rarely cooked for herself, preferring to eat out.

Most lunchtimes she ate with clients of the company for whom she worked. Most evenings she ate either snacks while working at home or went out with friends. How different her life-style was now from her mother's!

This visit home, as always, her mother had probed gently into her personal life. What she wanted to know was if Hannah had fallen in love. Hannah had gently evaded her questions, not because she resented them but simply because she didn't know how to explain to her mother that falling in love for her was something that just wasn't going to happen. She had seen what the pressures of modern living did to too many of her friends' relationships to risk such intimacy herself, and vicars' daughters weren't like the rest of the female population, they either revolted and went completely wild or, like Hannah herself, they lived by a set of rules and regulations, so totally out of step with modern mores as to be archaic.

Not that either parent had ever put any pressure on Hannah to conform to special standards different from those of her peers, but she and the boys, most especially Hannah herself, had grown up desperately aware of how very vulnerable their father was to public opinion. While it might be all very well for the daughter of the local entrepreneur to be out discoing at fourteen years old, while the local landlord's daughter might have her name splashed all over the gossip press with impunity, and while other stalwarts of the Women's Guild might discreetly let slip that their daughters were involved in intimate relationships which did not include a wedding ring, Hannah was in no doubt at all that the local community as a whole would not only strongly disapprove of any such behaviour on *her* part, but would also carry that disapproval to the ears of her father, and, quite simply, Hannah had never felt able to put that burden on him.

Now, of course, she was living away from home and in London, where she had her own airy apartment in the refurbished docklands area, and she had grown into the habit of evading intimacy, preferring solitude to 'coupledom', so that she automatically fended off those men who did approach her sexually. Fair-mindedly, she had to admit that her single state wasn't entirely because of her parents.

There had also been her career. She had worked single-mindedly to achieve the high position she now held: consultant to one of the managers of a very small but well-established firm of financial experts. The genteel poverty of her childhood wasn't something she had enjoyed, she felt ashamed to admit now.

There had been times when she had envied other children their possessions, their toys, their spending money, even though with wisdom and security she could appreciate that the gifts she had received from her parents had been of far more value than mere material possessions. Even so, she had been left with a desire, almost a craving, for financial security, not the kind of security that came from marriage to a wealthy man, but the kind of security she could earn for herself.

The village wasn't busy. It was half-day closing. Hannah's mother had been surprised when she had telephoned early in the week to say that she was taking a couple of days off, and to ask if it was convenient for her to come home. She hadn't said anything then about Linda's desperate telephone call to her the previous day, begging her to advise her.

Linda Askew was the daughter of a local businessman. She and Hannah had been at school together, and their friendship had been established then. The only child of wealthy parents, Linda had chosen not to go on to university as Hannah had, but her parents' death in a car crash two years ago had revealed the shocking fact that the business was virtually bankrupt. In order to pay off her father's outstanding debts, Linda had sold virtually everything.

Forced to confront the necessity of earning her own living, she had bought a small property in the village and decided to use her interest and expertise in various forms of needlework to establish a small shop. The business had done well. Linda was a sympathetic and caring person. She had a flair for designing, and her tapestries had become much sought after.

An approach from a glossy magazine had resulted in them marketing one of her tapestries as a special offer to their readers. The offer had been wildly successful, and it was because of the funds she had received via this offer that Linda found that she had now run into problems with the Inland Revenue. They had confronted her with a demand for tax which, she had told Hannah tearfully, she simply could not pay.

Having previously dealt with her own accounting system, she had not known whom to turn to, and so Hannah had offered to come down to the village and go with her on her appointment to see the tax inspector. Because it was half-day closing, it was relatively easy for her to park in the main street of the village.

Checking that the burglar alarm was in place and firmly locking her door, Hannah walked briskly towards Linda's shop, not going to the front door but going the full length of the row of stone-built houses and then round the back, past the long, narrow gardens, where the richness of the autumn-hued flowers was just beginning to take over from the brilliant blaze of summer.

Linda was waiting for her by her back door. She ushered Hannah inside quickly and said breathlessly, 'I've got the coffee on. I didn't know whether you'd want a cup or . . .'

'I'd love one,' Hannah told her. 'I can drink it while I go through your papers. What time exactly is the appointment?'

Linda told her and Hannah checked her watch. That left her a good hour to run through the figures, which should be ample time. She found the error quickly enough, a simple mistake in adding up, which had resulted in Linda paying less than the amount of tax that she ought to have paid the previous year.

'Oh, no,' Linda said, sitting down, her face going pale. 'Oh, Hannah, what on earth am I going to do?'

'It's not as bad as it looks,' Hannah assured her. 'I've just checked back into your previous year's figures, and you seem to have made a trading loss, but from what I can see, you actually paid tax.'

'Well, yes,' Linda agreed, frowning slightly as she scanned the figures Hannah was indicating. 'You see, I got the demand and I . . . well, I just paid it.'

Hannah hid a tiny grimace. 'Well, at the end of the day, I suspect you will probably find that you only owe the Inland Revenue a very small sum of money indeed,' she said soothingly. 'What we need to do now is to put all these figures in front of the inspector.'

'Oh, Hannah, you must think me an absolute idiot,' Linda said ruefully, as they finished their coffee and Hannah collected all the papers, folding them neatly and inserting them into a spare file she was carrying in her black leather briefcase. 'I don't know why it is, but the sight of a column of figures always throws me into an absolute panic. I always used to envy you. You were always top of the class in maths.'

'And you were always top in domestic science,' Hannah reminded her, 'whereas I was still sewing the same grubby scrap of fabric in the fifth form as I was in the third.'

Her comment lightened Linda's tension, as she had intended it to do, and the other girl laughed.

'Yes, I suppose we all have our weaknesses and our strong points,' she agreed.

The tax office was in the local county town, and when Hannah suggested that they both went in her car Linda agreed willingly.

'I'm still driving Dad's old Jag,' she told her. 'It's on its last legs now, really, but I can't afford to replace it, even though it guzzles petrol at an appalling rate. Mack at the garage somehow or other manages to keep it going for me, I don't know how.'

Without taking her eyes off the road, Hannah said *sotto voce,* 'A labour of love, perhaps.'

Linda flushed, and Hannah reflected on her mother's comments that the village grapevine was reporting that Linda and Ian Macdonald were 'getting involved'.

'He's been marvellous since Dad died,' Linda said quietly. 'I don't really know what I'd have done without him. It was he who suggested that I bought the shop, and he gave me trade references when I first set up in business. He even offered to guarantee my loan with the bank, but I couldn't let him do that. He's away at the moment,' she gave a slight sigh, 'a family funeral in Edinburgh.'

Hence the frantic call to her, Hannah recognised. The county town wasn't busy. Hannah knew where the local Inland Revenue offices were and parked her car deftly in the nearest car park. Several people eyed her businesslike suit and crisp, authoritative manner as she and Linda waited to cross the road.

She looked out of place here in the quiet mellowness of the old stone town. Young mothers in jeans and sweatshirts pushed prams or held the hands of toddlers. Older women in tweeds and sensible shoes, carrying shopping baskets, eyed her curiously. A group of youths stopped and stared, one of them whistling at her. Hannah ignored them. She was used to attracting attention.

Long ago she had learned the necessity of playing down her looks. In the career she had chosen, to look feminine in the way she herself looked feminine was not an asset. The full softness of her mouth made men think thoughts that were not at all business-like. The high curves of her breasts concealed by her silk shirt and the businesslike cut of her suit jacket caused male concentration to wander, and in the early days of her career she had encountered more than her fair share of sexual harrassment, before a kindly and far more worldly colleague had taken her on one side and pointed out that in their line of business, a lushly feminine figure such as hers was definitely not an asset—not if she wished to be taken seriously, that was. And so Hannah had learned to disguise the narrowness of her waist and the fullness of her breasts.

She had learned to adopt a severe, almost cold

expression. She had learned to modulate her voice so that it never betrayed any emotion. She had had her hair cut and kept it straight and sleek in a businesslike bob, and most of all she had learned to control her terrible betraying temper, to distance herself from the slights and snubs she had endured in the early days of working her way up the career ladder.

She had come a long way from the girl she had been when she had first left university, but there was still a long, long way to go. She thought about the new job she had applied for. She had heard about it on the grapevine, a prestige appointment as vice-president of a small but extremely highly geared financial services group. The post would involve working very closely with the chairman of the group, someone whom Hannah had never met, but whom she had heard much about. His name featured frequently in the pages of the *Financial Times*. It was spoken with awe over the lunch tables of their small, élite world.

Silas Jeffreys was a man who guarded his privacy with the utmost stringency. She had never even seen a photograph of him, never read a word of gossip about his private life, never even met the man, but what she had heard of his reputation, what she knew of the way he ran his business, told her how much she wanted to work with him. It would be like sitting at the feet of a master.

She had applied for the job a week ago. She had an interview on Monday, a good sign. She could feel cautiously hopeful. Her qualifications and work experience were good, but there were still intelligent and otherwise sane men who did not believe that women could work in finance, and she had no way of knowing if he was one of that number.

No amount of discreet probing could elicit enough information for her to draw a composite picture of the man, which was aggravating to someone like Hannah who had trained herself to have a neat, orderly mind and to keep her mind empty of clutter but full of information.

As they walked into the building, she and Linda were moving at the same pace, but by the time they had entered the reception area Hannah noticed that Linda was lagging slightly behind her. She hid a small smile. After all, her friend wasn't the only person to be intimidated by the vast anonymity of the Revenue offices.

The girl on reception was young and smiled warmly at them. Obviously she hadn't been in her job very long yet, Hannah reflected cynically, as she turned enquiringly to Linda, asking her for the name of the tax officer they were due to see.

Linda had it written down, and she handed the piece of paper over to the girl nervously.

'Oh, yes, he's on the fifth floor,' the girl told her, giving them another warm smile.

The lift was old and creaked as it moved slowly upwards. A symbol of the tax system itself, or simply symbolic of a careful husbanding of national resources? Hannah wondered, as she and Linda stood silently side by side. Her friend was very nervous. Hannah wanted to tell her not to be, but she knew that it wouldn't do the slightest good. She wanted to tell her that tax officials were only human, after all, capable of standards that were good, bad and indifferent, just like anyone else, and merely trained to appear distant and sharply suspicious of the motives of the public. However, Linda was very vulnerable and emotional where her weakness over figures was concerned, and Hannah suspected that, like somebody with a phobia about visiting the dentist, no amount of reassurance from someone else would tend to lessen her apprehension.

They found the office down a long corridor, a small boxlike room furnished with a basic desk, a chair behind it and then two other chairs in front of it. Behind the desk was a set of filing cabinets and some open shelves full of bulging files, books and other papers. Hannah could see all this through the glass partition of the door as she knocked briefly on it and waited for the young man working behind the desk to lift his head and invite them in.

He did so very politely, and Hannah read in the grimness behind the polite words and the tiredness she could see in his eyes the kind of strain that comes from long, long hours of work, when the worker knows that no matter how many hours that he or she puts in the work itself will never diminish. Hannah introduced herself, firmly shaking his hand and advising him that she would be representing Linda.

She sat down and explained calmly and concisely that an error had occurred, but that it was merely an error and not an attempt to defraud the Revenue. The inspector looked unconvinced, which was no more than Hannah had expected. Linda, however, shot her a nervous, agitated glance, quickly bursting into a muddled explanation of how the error had first occurred.

The interview lasted far longer than the young inspector could have anticipated. Hannah was tireless and relentless in putting forward Linda's case, checking every move that the young man made, calmly and coolly putting forward a very strong defence of Linda's errors. Hannah saw him glance surreptitiously at his watch. A date? she wondered, seeing the tiny frown touch his forehead.

His telephone rang and he excused himself to answer it. He listened for a few seconds, and then said tersely, 'Yes, thank you. Can you ask him to wait down there for me, please?'

Whoever was at the other end of the line said something else, and then the tax inspector said, 'Oh, well, if he's already on his way up . . .'

As soon as he had replaced the receiver, Hannah said smoothly, 'I'm sorry we're taking so much of your time, but you can understand Linda's concern over the whole matter.'

'We, too, have been concerned,' the tax inspector responded tersely, but he wasn't looking at her, Hannah realised. His attention wasn't focused on them the way it had been before. Instead he was looking at the door.

They heard the footsteps on the uncarpeted corridor, long before the door opened. Male footsteps, firm and very, very sure of themselves. The door opened, but Hannah didn't turn round to look to see who had come in. Whoever the visitor was, she suspected from the look of strain on the tax inspector's face that he wasn't entirely welcome.

She wondered if it was a more senior inspector come to check on the young man's progress, and decided that she was right in her assumption when she heard him saying awkwardly, 'I'm sorry, I'm not quite finished here.'

Seeing an opportunity to put Linda's case before a more senior authority, Hannah turned toward the newcomer, only just managing to suppress her shock as she saw him for the first time.

Her first impression was that he made the small room seem even smaller. He was leaning on the back wall of the office, his arms crossed negligently in front of him, his tall, broad-shouldered frame encased in a suit that Hannah's practised business eye recognised immediately as coming from Savile Row. The fabric alone must have cost a fortune—that kind of wool and silk mixture was unbelievably expensive, as she knew to her cost.

His suit was charcoal grey—the same colour as his eyes, she noticed absently—his shirt impossibly white, the cuffs fastened with plain, expensive gold links, the old-fashioned kind of double links in wafer-thin old gold. Instead of the uniform striped tie, though, his was a bright, sharp red. She focused on it, studying it, a tiny frown touching her forehead, and as though he sensed her confusion amusement curled the corners of his mouth.

Hannah didn't see the amusement, though; she was too busy wondering in outraged disappointment how a tax official, no matter how lofty, came to be wearing a suit which her astute brain told her had probably cost upward of one and half thousand pounds.

Behind her, she heard the young inspector make a murmured comment which she didn't quite catch. She suspected the young man was fully aware that Linda had had no intention of deliberately defrauding the Revenue, and she also suspected that he was being over severe with her friend to warn her in future to keep a better grip on the financial side of her business. But Linda was beginning to look pale and sick, and Hannah had tired of the unchallenging game of outmanoeuvring the young inspector.

Now, as she raised her glance from the older man's tie to his face, she went crisply through the small saga once again, this time to the older man, pointing out that there were considerable losses for Linda's first year of trading which she in her ignorance had not claimed back, and that these more than offset the amount she owed in unpaid tax.

There was an odd silence in the room after she had delivered her argument. She saw the look the older man gave the younger: grave and considering. The younger man coloured slightly, opened his mouth to say something and then closed it again at a tiny shake of the older man's head, which Hannah only just caught. She took advantage of it, adding smoothly, turning back to address the younger inspector, 'In fact, if you *had* checked through the first year's accounts, you would have seen that there were trading losses.'

His colour deepened, and he looked uncomfortably over Hannah's head towards the older man.

How much older? Ten years—a little more? He was somewhere in his early to mid-thirties, Hannah estimated, with features that almost had too much visual impact. His skin was dark as though tanned, but she suspected the olive tinge was natural, hinting at perhaps Spanish or Italian blood somewhere in his background, his nose aquiline and emphasising the arrogance of his profile. High cheekbones jutted beneath the grey glitter of his eyes, his hair thick and very dark, immaculately shaped to his long skull.

Now for the first time he spoke directly to her, his voice deep and paced, without holding any inflection other than a certain malicious silkiness as he pointed out, 'But surely that's *your* job as this young lady's accountant to point those losses out to the Revenue, not theirs to point them out to you. The Revenue is hard pressed enough as it is, undermanned to an extent that in private industry would be considered criminal; its staff are expected to produce miracles and are constantly under siege from those sections of the population that deem it—er . . . unjust that they should abide by the taxation laws of this country, while of course expecting to have the full benefit from being a British citizen. Besides, I think you've tormented this young man enough, don't you?' he asked her wryly, wringing an unwary start of surprise from her.

'An error appears to have been made—on both sides,' he continued. 'I suggest that you leave your papers here so that we can have time to go through in a less . . . combustible atmosphere. The Revenue takes no sides. It simply seeks to fulfil its duty in ensuring that the country's citizens pay their full dues.'

For the first time in a long, long time Hannah felt

her colour rise. She was being told off . . . reminded very promptly and calmly of the stresses the young inspector was under . . . made to feel almost childishly unkind in her clear-cut definitions of his errors. She felt small and mean, and just a tiny little bit ashamed of herself.

Which was surely completely ludicrous. If she hadn't come with Linda to help and support her, her poor friend would have been in a state of complete panic and would have probably been browbeaten into paying out tax which she simply did not owe.

She opened her mouth to say as much, and then closed it again. Taking her critic's comments personally would not do Linda's case any good. Summoning the self-control she had taught herself so hardily over the years, she curved her mouth into a cool, professional smile and said in an equally cool and professional voice, 'Of course. We'll leave it with you, then.'

And she got up and shook hands briskly across the desk with the younger man, waiting for Linda to do the same.

For some reason, as she walked the small distance to the door, she didn't offer her hand to the older man; and she even found that she was deliberately keeping a greater distance between them than was at all necessary.

Why? Because she found his sexuality intimidating? Nonsense. Why on earth should she? What was there to be frightened of? That he might try and pounce on her? She stifled a mirthless laugh. Hardly . . . On looks alone he could have women beating a path to his door, and was hardly likely to find it necessary to do something so unprofessional as to make a pass at her. So she stopped at the door and turned round, gravely proffering him her hand. She saw the smile that twitched at his mouth and frowned, wondering what had caused it. Not her, surely? She bristled a little at the thought and gave him a clear, frosty look from her tawny eyes.

'Thank goodness that's over,' Linda breathed as soon as they were out of earshot of the office. 'What do you think will happen?'

'I'm sure you have nothing to worry about,' Hannah soothed her, 'but if you're at all worried, just give me a ring at the flat. You've got the number.'

The late summer sunshine was casting long shadows as they walked out of the building.

Just as they were about to cross the road, Linda remembered that she had some letters to post, so they retraced their footsteps back to the post office.

When they returned to the car park, Hannah discovered an elegant Daimler saloon was parked next to her own car. She looked at it enviously, wondering who it belonged to.

'It's lovely, isn't it?' Linda said wryly. 'I only hope for its owner's sake that it has better fuel consumption than my old one.'

When Hannah stopped her car outside Linda's shop, Linda invited her in for supper but Hannah shook her head. She would be late enough as it was, and she had some reading up to do on the Jeffreys Group before her interview on Monday.

'What a pity you couldn't have taken a longer break,' Linda commiserated as they said goodbye. 'You must miss Dorset . . .'

'Yes, I do,' Hannah agreed honestly—an admission she would never have made to any of her colleagues who were such dedicated city dwellers. There were times when she felt almost claustrophobic in London, but living virtually on the river helped to banish that feeling, although nothing could ever really replace the spaciousness and rural beauty of her parents' home village.

'Unfortunately, London is where the jobs are. London and other capital cities.'

She wondered what Linda would say if she told her she was taking a special language course in Japanese; not that she intended to go and work in Japan, but the world was shrinking every day and the Japanese money markets were fast-growing business areas. One had to think of the future . . .

'Don't you ever envy the girls we grew up with, Hannah?' Linda asked her a little wistfully, her hand on the open passenger door of the car. 'I mean, they're all married now with children . . . families . . .'

'Not at all,' Hannah told her crisply. 'I'm not decrying marriage, Linda, but how many of those girls ever fulfilled their true potential? Oh, I'm not saying that being a wife and mother isn't fulfilling . . . of course it is, but I can't help wondering how many of those girls will turn round in ten years' time and find themselves alone, their marriages broken up and themselves the sole breadwinner, and how many of them then will regret not having trained for a career . . . in not having some sense of themselves, apart from their husbands and children.

'I prefer to rely on myself, rather than to rely on others,' she added firmly. 'It's much safer.'

Linda's mouth twisted a little bitterly. 'And that's a major consideration for our generation, isn't it? Safety. Have you ever noticed how much the word "safe" occurs in our conversations? We're almost obsessed by it.'

'With every good reason,' Hannah pointed out calmly. 'The world—today is a very dangerous place, made dangerous by we who inhabit it.'

She gave her friend a final smile, and when Linda had closed the door and disappeared inside her home she set the car in motion again, heading for London.

CHAPTER TWO

'HANNAH, where the devil are those figures on Hanson I asked you for last week?'

Refusing to react to the biting, bullying tone of her boss's voice, Hannah went calmly to his desk and removed a file, which she handed to him without showing any signs of either chagrin or triumph.

This was one of the main reasons she had applied for the Jeffreys' job. Ever since Brian Howard had been head-hunted by the directors, and appointed into a senior managerial post with the company, he had made her a target for his prejudice against her sex. A prejudice, that was, of her sex working in the same professional field as himself.

When he'd first joined the company, he had mistaken Hannah for one of the secretaries; his manner towards her had been insulting in the extreme and, as Hannah had told him coldly at the time, she sincerely felt for the secretarial staff if his behaviour towards her was indicative of the kind of sexual harassment *they* had to endure.

He had resented the tone she had taken with him, resented her sheer skill in her work and the professionalism that would not allow her to betray how much she disliked working for him.

He was forever needling her, criticising her and generally trying to put her down. And Hannah had resolved to herself several months ago that it would be sensible for her to look for another job. She was not a girl who believed in taking her problems to others, nor expecting them to solve them for her. The man was at fault, but since she knew quite well that what he wanted was a confrontation, whereby he could bully and browbeat her into feminine defensiveness and retreat, if possible accompanied by her loss of temper and, even better, her tears, she knew that to try and reason with him as she might have done with another man would be a sheer waste of time.

He resented her and he feared—not her—but her intelligence, her calm air of authority, her sheer ability.

Confrontation was not Hannah's way; she had tried it too often with her brothers as a child and lost. Nor did she intend to go behind his back and solicit the support of others. She preferred to handle the situation in her own way.

It had come as an unpleasant shock to realise what other members of her sex had to endure in the workplace. When she had said as much to one of the senior secretaries in an unguarded moment, the other girl had grimaced, and said, 'You don't know the half of it! Talk about pandering to the male ego . . . Some of them are sweeties and the worst you can say about them is that they haven't bothered to keep up with the new technology and that they expect their secretaries to do their work for them, and to keep quiet about their contributions when the plaudits are being handed out. But that's the *best* of them. The worst——' She had rolled her eyes and added grimly, 'I advise every junior secretary I train to make it plain right from the start where they stand when it comes to sexual harassment.'

'But how?' Hannah had asked, remembering how hard she had found it to get it through her boss's arrogant conceit that she found his advances repulsive.

'Oh, it's not easy, but there are ways. No provocative clothing, no flirtatious or misinterpretable remarks, unless you know the guy on the receiving end is going to take them the right way. And if you do get someone who steps out of line . . . well, depending on how far out of line he is, there are one or two tricks of the trade to make him see the error of his ways. Spilling his coffee over him, dropping a couple of files where it's going to hurt, mentioning his wife and saying you think your mother knows her.'

Even though she had laughed, Hannah had been appalled that such measures were necessary.

Now she waited as he studied the figures she had given him, his small mouth pursing meanly. He put down the papers and leaned across her desk, bracing his hands on the edge of it, a threatening sexual stance, which Hannah ignored.

'Two days off this week. Another off on Monday. Got a boyfriend, have we?'

Hannah bristled mentally at the overt prurience in his voice, but didn't lift her head from her work.

Her boss was balding and forty-odd, his body running to fat. He had a penchant for strong aftershaves which were unpleasant at close quarters. He was well-groomed, as one would expect of a man in his position, but Hannah reflected that it was more due to his wife than to him. The wife whom he openly boasted about keeping short of money at home . . . jocularly adding that it was the best place for women to be, while leering at the office junior as she whisked past in her fashionable short skirt.

Hannah detested him and all men like him, but she was wise enough to know that no amount of protesting would change his attitude.

She was glad when her telephone rang, making it unnecessary for her to answer his questions. At least it was Friday, and she had the whole weekend in which to prepare herself for Monday's interview.

When she was at home in her docklands apartment, Hannah dressed completely differently from the way she did for work. Jeans and sweatshirts were the order of the day, while she worked happily on decorating the apartment more in line with her own tastes than those of the builder.

She had opted for one of the more expensive apartments, with a generous balcony area and marvellous views of the Thames.

On Saturday morning, drawn outside by the sun, she ate her breakfast sitting by the balcony, lazily watching the world and his wife go by—most of them apparently driving bright scarlet Porsches, and wearing clothes from a very small and select group of designers.

'Yuppies', the media designated them with fiendish joy, but to Hannah, who was part of them professionally and yet apart from them personally, they sometimes seemed to be a sad, uncertain group, huddled together clone-like for comfort, desperate to conform to their own rigidly set standards. But then she allowed fair-mindedly that any group must seem like that to those on the outside.

She rested her chin in her hands as she stared out across the Thames, busy with craft as people made the most of the sunshine.

She ate the rest of her croissant, bought from the small specialist baker who had opened in the elegant shopping arcade not far from her apartment, acknowledging that she was lucky in her tall slenderness in that she never had to worry about putting on extra pounds.

Her eldest brother Matt had called at the apartment just after she'd moved in. He had been making an overnight stop in London, en route for Alaska and the pipeline whose constructions he had been heavily involved in.

'Very swish,' he had approved, grinning at her, as he inspected the stark black and white décor and furniture. 'Not much like home, though, is it?'

'It isn't meant to be,' Hannah had told him sharply, not liking the hint of amusement she sensed beneath his admiration.

Was that why she had almost deliberately set out to soften the harsh lines of the apartment's design, by bringing in rich textiles, silk damasks in scarlet and gold, India rugs that warmed the bare floorboards?

And in her bedroom she had given way fully to the imaginative side of her nature, the side she normally kept strictly under control, falling for and buying some French bedroom furniture in smooth, strong cherrywood.

The bed had high scrolled head and foot-boards

that made her think rather fancifully, when she lay in it looking out at the river, that she was lying in her own private barge, perhaps waiting for the tide to take her upriver to the heart of the city, or downriver and out to sea like an Elizabethan buccaneer.

The bed had a rich blue, silk damask quilted eider-down and matching spread; the silk had cost a fortune and she had wondered if she was a little mad after she had committed herself to its purchase, but there was something about the sensation of the silk, about the richness of its colour, about the sheer luxury of the fabric, that was worth every penny she had spent.

Curled up in the Lloyd loom chair she had filched from her bedroom at home, she studied the fact sheets she had assembled.

The Jeffreys Group had been started as a single cell company almost fifteen years before by Silas Jeffreys, who had seen an opening selling financial services to his fellow ex-graduates as they found their way in the business world. He had advised them on their tax affairs, their pensions, their investments; his financial acumen was so keen that he had been retained by several small, successful companies to reorganise their financial departments, and so his own business had grown.

He was one of the few new-wave financiers who did not feel it necessary to operate from New York as well as London, although he had been approached by various American concerns as a consultant.

The share crisis which had stunned worldwide stockmarkets in 1987 had left him unscathed, which had added to his aura of mystique.

Hannah put the papers to one side and thought of the people she knew by repute who worked for his organisation, all of them with formidable reputations. Jeffreys Group never head-hunted staff—it never needed to. The prestige of working for it was such that Silas Jeffreys could choose his own workforce from among the best financial brains in the country.

Would *she* be eligible to join that number? She pressed her hand to her stomach to quell the unfamiliar sensation of butterflies fluttering there.

Until now she hadn't admitted even to herself how important getting this job was. She had developed caution during her teens when she had discovered how much her enthusiasm for maths set her apart from her peers . . . Seeing how much they, especially her male peers, resented her success and her enthusiasm, she hadn't allowed herself to want anything too much. She could vividly remember as a teenager the excitement of being invited out on a date and then finding that the boy concerned didn't share her thirst for knowledge, her determination to use her talents to the full.

Was it then that she had started to teach herself to make a choice? To accept that, no matter what the media hyped, it wasn't possible to 'have it all?'

Among her acquaintances there were several couples with high-profile careers and marriages which seemed to thrive on busy schedules and frantic efforts to spend time together; they were happy and fulfilled, these energetic, busy couples who filled every moment of their lives, but Hannah wasn't sure if she possessed the ability to match such diversification, whether she had it in herself to make a success of marriage and a career. The men she had known had demanded too much from her, making her back off from them, making her fear that they would try to woo her away from her career.

She would like to be one of the enviable few who had it all: a satisfying career, plus a partner with whom she could genuinely share the joys and disappointments of her life, who would genuinely accept her as his equal, who would understand her desire to be part of the busy, thriving world of finance. And yet someone who at the same time understood her nostalgic yearning for a home such as the home her parents had built: comfortable, welcoming . . . a home where muddy boots and muddy paws were equally welcome, a home where children thrived, a garden full of sunshine in summer and snow in winter, comfortable rooms full of old furniture. And it was this ambiguity within her that insisted she make choices, that insisted that for her a career and marriage could not go hand in hand.

It might be different if she had ever met a man who mattered . . . a man so essential to her life that he would be the very core of it, and yet instinctively she feared that dependence, that emotional needing.

She closed her eyes, impatient of the deeply romantic vein within her that she preferred to ignore, and was stunned by the immediacy with which her imagination recreated for her the features of a certain tax official.

So, he had an openly visual masculine face, a male aura that had been hard to ignore, a subtle awareness of himself that had been vaguely challenging, giving her the sensation that he was daring her to react to him.

He was probably married with half a dozen children, and a lover tucked away discreetly somewhere, she told herself cynically, banishing his image. It was her mother's fault that she was suffering this mood of introspection . . . her loving, old-fashioned mother with her talk of weddings and babies, and her thinly veiled anxiety that she, her daughter, was never going to produce grandchildren for her to coo over and boast about.

She had four brothers, for heaven's sake, Hannah thought pettishly. Let them produce grandchildren . . .

She had received several casual invitations from friends for events over the weekend, but she had turned them all down, wanting to concentrate on planning her interview strategy. Besides, there was a Beethoven concert on the radio on Sunday evening which she wanted to hear.

She went to bed early, wishing she could subdue the restless sensation of dissatisfaction which had invaded her. It was counter-productive and dangerous. There was no room for it in her life. Especially not now when she faced what was probably the most challenging interview of her career.

On Monday morning she was up at her normal time. Her interview was at eleven o'clock, which left her plenty of time to get ready. She showered and washed her hair, blowdrying it into its smooth bob, and dressing carefully in a cool cream satin shirt and a new suit in navy with a chalk stripe, severely cut and formidably businesslike.

Navy tights, Jourdan pumps, her expensive navy leather briefcase. On her wrist, her discreet gold watch. The gold ear-rings the boys had bought her for Christmas in her ears. A light spray of the cool fresh perfume she favoured, just to let the interviewer know that, while she had no intentions of trading on her femininity, neither was she in the slightest ashamed of it.

She was lucky in the excellence of her skin, which required little make-up. She uncapped her new lipstick, a soft red, which the salesgirl had enthused over, but which, once she had it on, seemed to draw attention to her mouth in a way she was not sure she liked, even though there was nothing vibrant or striking about the colour. She hesitated to wipe it off, frowning a little and then deciding she was being over-critical, not seeing in her reflection what a man would notice straight away—and that was that the subtle gleam of the lipstick drew attention to the unexpectedly vulnerable fullness of her mouth, throwing it into challenging contrast with her businesslike appearance.

Just a mere brush of matt dark green eyeshadow to shape her eyes, and blusher to highlight her cheekbones, and then she was ready.

She hadn't varnished her nails, which she kept short and well-buffed, and a small, fine gold ring which had belonged to a maternal great-aunt was her only piece of jewellery apart from her watch and ear-rings.

Before leaving, she stood on her balcony and took several calming deep breaths, concentrating all her mental energies within herself, gathering herself up for the ordeal ahead. And then she was ready.

She wasn't driving her car, not having wanted to risk being unable to find a parking spot. The taxi she had ordered arrived on time, and she saw the driver give her an appreciative male look as she stepped into it. She ignored the look and crisply gave him his directions.

The Jeffreys Group had its offices, not in one of the high modern office blocks, but in a Georgian house in an elegant terrace of such houses set round one of London's smaller squares.

The garden in the middle was lushly green, the trees throwing welcome shadows on to the footpath. The railings that guarded the square were painted black and tipped with gold; and as the taxi stopped alongside them to allow her to alight Hannah noticed a small gothic gazebo, almost hidden by the foilage, its walls painted green, only the pewter shimmer of its bell-shaped roof betraying its presence.

The garden had a padlocked gate, and inside someone was working, tirelessly weeding.

Although there was really no similarity between them whatsoever, for some reason the small garden made Hannah think of her home, and her mother, who loved the vicarage's rambling, overgrown garden almost as much as though it was an extra child.

The square was full of parked cars: expensive, gleaming cars with German pedigrees, almost uniformly dark in colour, apart from the occasional thrusting scarlet of a new Porsche or Ferrari.

The car parked outside the Group's front door was

a Daimler, the same colour as the one she had noticed in the car park at home, Hannah recognised in passing.

The Georgian door was painted black and decorated with traditional brass knocker and handle. Above it, the delicacy of the Adam fanlight caught Hannah's eye, and she hesitated, uncertain as to whether to knock or simply walk in. As she waited, the door opened and she realised that someone must be watching her. The thought made her feel slightly uncomfortable. She stepped into the cool darkness of the tiled hallway and found a smiling receptionist waiting to greet her.

'Hannah Maitland?' she questioned, and when Hannah nodded, she said pleasantly, 'If you would just like to wait in the library. It's down the corridor, first door on your right. You're a few minutes early for your appointment. Would you like a cup of tea or coffee while you're waiting?'

Hannah shook her head. She was too nervous to need any added stimulation.

Thanking the receptionist, she followed her directions and found that the library was exactly that: a welcoming, faintly musty room with leather chairs and mahogany bookshelves, stacked with leather-bound volumes. The carpet on the floor was Persian and beautifully faded. The original Adam fireplace had been retained, and, even though Hannah suspected that the discreetly mellowed panelling along one wall probably concealed all manner of up-to-date computer and visual study equipment, it did not detract from the ambience of the room at all.

It was a room that spoke of comfort and mellowness . . . of a need to respect the proper order of things . . . of tradition and timelessness. It was a room that relaxed and reassured, she recognised sensitively.

She wasn't being interviewed by Silas Jeffreys himself, but by his deputy, which led her to suspect that this was just a weeding-out series of interviews.

She glanced surreptitiously at her watch. Three minutes to go. Her heart leapt as the door opened and then it leapt again, as she recognised the man who walked in, although for a far different reason.

To say that she was staggered to come face to face with the senior of the two tax officials from her county town, here of all places, was to grossly underestimate her feelings.

Her mouth dropped open as she stared at him in disbelief; her shock heightened by an odd feeling of fear and resentment. What was he doing here?

And then she knew. He was another contender for the job and a formidable opponent to her own chances, so her instincts told her.

He smiled at her as though coming face to face with her was an everyday occurrence, and once again she felt off balance and unnerved by his own very evident lack of reaction.

'What do you think?' he asked her pleasantly, and it took her several seconds to realise he was asking her opinion of their surroundings.

'It's . . . it's very cleverly designed,' she managed snappishly when she had recovered her composure. 'Relaxing and reassuring. Clients coming in here would immediately feel reassured about the probity of the Group.'

He shot her a thoughtful look. Hannah would almost have described it as an assessing look, were it not for the fact that the mere thought of him daring to assess her made her stiffen with rejection and irritation.

'You'll be going in for your interview in a moment.' He made the comment a statement rather than a question, and that added fuel to the fire of her resentment. 'What is it that appeals most to you about this position?' he questioned.

Hannah only just managed to stifle her gasp of fury.

'I think that's for the interviewer to ask and not you,' she told him pointedly, and then couldn't resist adding with a small grimace, 'I suppose there's no need to ask what you're doing here? Although surely,' she added with what she knew to be a touch of malice, 'it's rather dangerous for a man of your age to make such a major career move.'

She saw him start slightly, as if she had surprised him, and felt a fierce stab of pleasure, as though somehow the thought of having got the better of him, in however small a way, boosted her own self-confidence.

'What makes you think I'm contemplating a career move?' he asked her smoothly. eyebrows lifting in an interrogative manner.

'The mere fact that you're here,' she responded crisply. 'It's obvious, isn't it? What other purpose could there be in you, a tax official, appearing here in the offices of a private company? Unless, of course,' she added nastily, 'you've come to interview Mr Jeffreys about his personal tax affairs.'

He gave her a calm smile, which added to her growing irritation with him. His eyes crinkled a little at the corners, as though he was suppressing a desire to laugh. His whole manner towards her was so reminiscent of the lordly attitude adopted by her older brothers that she longed to react to his male arrogance in the same way as she had reacted to theirs as a little girl. Hadn't she learnt then, though, the uselessness of pitting her own much frailer strength against that of her much bigger and stronger brothers?

This man would have as little difficulty in fending off flaying fists and angry words as they had done. As she realised what she thinking, Hannah was furious with herself, just as furious as she had originally been with him.

What on earth was she doing, allowing this man to trick her into losing her temper and her self-control? Undermining the confidence of the other applicants for a position was surely one of the oldest tricks in the book, and she should have had more sense than to fall for it.

The door to the library opened and the receptionist from the front entrance came in, starting a little as she realised that Hannah wasn't the only occupant in the room. She looked uncertainly from Hannah to her companion, as though not quite certain which one of them she should address.

The problem was solved for her when he turned his back and walked over to the bookshelves, studying their contents.

'If you'd like to come this way, please,' she said a little breathlessly to Hannah, more than half her attention still focused on the relaxed back of the other occupant of the room. Irritated by the way the girl couldn't take her attention off him and focus it on her, Hannah gave her a cool smile and swept towards the door, only just restraining herself from making some acid remark to her opponent.

The receptionist escorted her to a lift, discreetly hidden in the rear of the hallway.

'It will take you directly to the executive suite,' she told Hannah, 'and when you get there Mr Giles' secretary will be waiting for you.'

Gordon Giles was Silas Jeffreys' second-in-command, a man whose reputation was almost as formidable as that of Silas Jeffreys himself. Hannah felt a tremor of nervousness start in the tip of her stomach as she got into the lift. It was silly to let herself be unnerved by that wholly unexpected and wholly unwanted second encounter with the tax official.

How had he heard about this job? she wondered acidly, as the lift slowed smoothly to a halt and the door opened automatically.

Gordon Giles' secretary was about her own age, a pleasant, intelligent-looking brunette, who smiled warmly at her as she escorted her to Gordon Giles' office.

Gordon Giles himself was not as intimidating as Hannah had expected. A tall, thin, slightly stooping man in his early fifties, he greeted her with a warm smile and a firm handshake, offering her a seat with a faintly old-world air of courtesy that had nothing sexist in it and was merely an expression of what her mother would term 'good manners'.

He started the interview without any preamble, remarking, as Hannah herself already knew, that her qualifications were excellent.

'Your work experience is a little more limited than that of most of the other applicants,' he told her quite freely, 'but that needn't necessarily count against you.'

He went on to discuss various aspects of the job, should Hannah actually get it, making the odd note as she answered his questions.

'Now,' he said firmly, pushing aside his papers and studying her thoughtfully, 'please don't take this amiss, but your personal life . . . just how free are you to travel? Silas wants an assistant whose personal life and responsibilities are fluid enough to enable him or her to travel with him. He has recently bought a house in the country and he spends two, sometimes three days a week working from there. As his personal assistant you would be required to stay overnight there and so be available to work with him. Would that cause you any problems?' he asked her directly.

Hannah shook her head, knowing from the tone of his voice that she had nothing to fear or resent in telling him the truth, and that it was not prurient curiosity or any sexist attitude that motivated his questions.

'I live alone,' she told him calmly, 'and I'm completely free to adapt to whatever arrangements Mr Jeffreys wishes to make.'

'And the thought of spending two, possibly three, out of every five working days out of London doesn't worry you?' he persisted.

'Not at all,' Hannah told him honestly. 'I was brought up in the country and miss it. To work in London and in the country would be like having the best of both worlds.'

'Good. There is one other point I feel I should mention, and that is something you may or may not know.'

Hannah waited, not quite sure of what was to come, a little perturbed by the faint frown that touched his forehead, his almost fatherly note of concern in his voice, when he told her, 'Silas isn't married, and while of course I can totally and completely vouch for him both as an employer and as a man, you might feel that I had been less than honest with you, if at a future date we were to offer you the job. I'm simply saying this now to avoid wasting both your time and ours.'

He glanced down at the files that lay on his desk and said simply, 'I see from your CV that your father is a vicar.' Hannah immediately caught on. She suppressed the tiny flash of irritation that burned through her. How many times in the past had people on discovering her father's career made incorrect judgements about her—and yet, to be fair, she had to admit that Gordon Giles had said nothing that was either offensive or unrealistic.

'I'm not someone who is given to over-imaginative flights of fancy,' she told him swiftly. 'The knowledge that Mr Jeffreys isn't married and that I should be spending a couple of nights a week under his roof causes me no concern whatsoever. In fact,' she added in a slightly more wry tone, 'I should imagine the apprehension, if there is any, would be all on his side.'

Her remark drew an appreciative laugh from Gordon Giles.

'I'm glad you have a sense of humour,' he told her. 'Silas will appreciate that.'

Will—Hannah pounced mentally on the small slip and then wondered if it was perhaps deliberate. She was taking nothing for granted. The interview seemed to have gone well, but she had no way of judging Gordon Giles' interview technique, since she had no knowledge of what had been said to the other interviewees.

She thought about the man downstairs and wondered how he would interview. He had an arrogance about him that made her think that he would not adjust well to working so directly under someone else. He had that air about him that suggested that he would want to be top dog.

There were several more questions, including the ones she had dreaded, about her reasons for leaving her existing employment. Hannah told him only that she had felt it was time for a career move and that hearing about this job on the grapevine had prompted her into applying for it.

He seemed quite satisfied with her response, asking her a few more general questions before standing up and indicating that the interview was over.

'We'll be in touch just as soon as we can,' he told her, shaking her hand firmly, and then using the intercom to summon his secretary.

Outside again in the sunlight, Hannah couldn't resist glancing back at the window to the library. Was he sitting in the chair she had just vacated now, answering the same questions she had answered? It was annoying how dangerously easily he seemed to have slipped into her thoughts, disturbing the calm serenity of them.

Since she had no car, she walked until she was able to hail a taxi. It was lunchtime, but she had no appetite either for food or for company, and so instead she went straight home. Once there, she had an odd impulse to pick up the telephone and ring her parents so that she could tell them all about her interview and seek their caring parental reassurance, but she quelled the impulse, deciding to wait until it was safer to talk to them about it, if and when she was called for a second interview. Safe. There it was again; that word appeared so frequently in her life, dictating her patterns of behaviour. Was that why she was so determined never to fall in love, because she knew deep down inside herself how very dangerous it would be for her, how very vulnerable she would be, if she ever gave her heart completely to someone?

She shivered a little and thought about him, grimacing as she realised whenever she thought of THE SENIOR TAX INSPECTOR, it was always somehow in capital letters. She suspected that safety was not something that figured very largely in his life plan, and that he would scorn people like her for their timidity. It annoyed her that she should be thinking about him again. She wondered how his interview had gone, and then acknowledged a little bleakly that he probably had far more chance of being called to a second interview than she did.

He had seemed almost amused by her reference to the fact that they were rivals for the same job, and that in itself was surely rather odd? If anything, she would have expected him to be resentful, or maybe even bitterly sceptical of her ability to fill such a post, but he had simply smiled, a genuine smile at that, and that rankled, making her wonder what he had found in her that she herself couldn't see that had caused him so much amusement.

Well, at least, whether she got the job or not, she was hardly likely to see him again, and as she headed for her room she wondered why that knowledge should cause a small pang of loneliness inside her.

CHAPTER THREE

TO HANNAH'S relief, she didn't have to wait long before hearing from Gordon Giles. A letter arrived in Wednesday morning's post, bearing the distinctive Jeffreys Group logo.

Hannah opened it with nervous fingers, almost holding her breath in trepidation as she did so.

The letter inside the envelope was written on expensive, thick cream vellum paper. It looked brief, and her heartbeat almost doubled. A polite note of regret, or a summons to another interview . . . which was it?

She unfolded it and read it, stunned to discover that it was neither, and then she read the brief, concise sentences again in case she had misinterpreted them the first time, but no, she hadn't. She was being offered the job as vice-president and personal assistant to Silas Jeffreys, at a salary that made her goggle, and with an impressive list of fringe benefits that included a company car.

She would give her Volvo to her parents, she decided headily. Her father complained in a good-natured way about the frailty and age of his old Ford, and would make good use of her sturdy, solid Volvo.

The final sentence of the letter contained the information that an appointment had been made for her to meet Silas Jeffreys on Friday at ten o'clock, and if she found she wasn't interested in accepting the job she was to telephone his secretary and advise her.

Hannah could hardly believe it. Dizzy with excitement, she wandered out on to her balcony, clutching the letter and her morning mug of coffee—her one indulgence in an otherwise exemplary healthy life-style.

She had got the job! She wanted to shout the news from her balcony, but as she stood there she realised bleakly that, even if she did, no one would care. None of her large circle of friends was close enough for her to have confided her plans to them. She had no lover to share her joy and excitement. Her parents would be thrilled for her, but their pleasure would be diminished by the distance that separated them.

Frowning slightly, Hannah wandered disconsolately back into her living-room. What was the matter with her? She had just got the job she yearned for, and instead of feeling a glowing sense of achievement her pleasure was tinged with loneliness and an awareness of that loneliness. Her aloneness had never bothered her before. In fact, she had cherished it. Why was she so aware of it now? It had nothing to do with a certain six foot odd, grey-eyed, predatory-looking male, did it?

Angry with herself for the direction of her thoughts, Hannah drank her coffee quickly, wondering a little grimly how *he* was feeling this morning. Disappointed because he hadn't got the job? Would he guess that *she* had got it? She felt a tiny savage kick of triumph, wishing that he could know. She had not missed the almost indulgent way he had looked at her, first in the tax offices and then in the library at the Jeffreys Group offices: indulgently and humorously, as though there was something about her that greatly amused him. Well, she wondered how amusing he would find it to discover that she had snatched the job from under his nose.

Telling herself sternly that her reactions were almost childish, she hurried to get ready for work. If she wasn't careful, she was going to be late; something so unprofessional as not to be even thought of.

All the way to her office her mind was busy with plans. She would give in her formal notice on Friday, after her interview with Silas Jeffreys. She would write to his secretary in her lunch hour today, confirming that she was accepting the job and would keep the appointment. She would ring her parents tonight to tell them the good news . . .

Friday came round very, very quickly indeed. Hannah had told her boss that she was taking the whole day off, as part of her holiday allocation.

He hadn't been pleased, but since Hannah had already forfeited one week's holiday at almost a moment's notice he had very little option but to agree, although he made it plain to her how much he disapproved.

Thanking her lucky stars that she wouldn't have to put up with him for much longer, Hannah got ready for her interview.

Some impulse she couldn't quite understand, but which had something to do with the rich, warm colours of the library where she had waited to be summoned for her interview, and, if she was honest, something to do with the way 'his' mouth had twitched a little as he surveyed her business suit with unhidden amusement, made her choose a dress from her wardrobe that she had bought on impulse and never worn.

It was made of soft red cashmere, the shade of red that went well with tawny hair, and shaped in classical lines that looked nothing on the hanger, but which fitted Hannah's body with a fluid elegance that made it worth every penny of the exorbitant price she had paid for it.

She had never worn it, simply because she considered it too feminine, too womanly, and thus not suitable for office wear. If she was honest, she had to admit that her decision had been influenced by the behaviour of her boss, who she had known would not have been able to resist making a sexist remark on seeing her in it.

It infuriated Hannah that, simply because she was not flat-chested, she should be forced to endure the kind of gratuitous and insulting remarks that men like him felt free to make if she wore anything that did not almost completely disguise the fullness of her breasts.

Deep down somewhere inside herself, she acknowledged that wearing the dress was probably some kind of test, as much for Silas Jeffreys as for herself.

Over it she wore a three-quarter-length black wool jacket, warm enough to withstand the slightly chill breeze that heralded the end of summer. It was only just September, but already Hannah, country born and bred, could smell the scents that preceded autumn.

She arrived promptly for her interview and was shown immediately to the executive lift and told that Silas Jeffreys' secretary would be waiting for her when the lift stopped.

She was, and she showed Hannah straight into his office, frowning a little as she realised it was empty.

'He said to show you straight in here. I'm sure he won't be a moment,' she apologised, her professionalism slipping a little as she allowed herself to frown, as though it was unusual for him not to be prompt.

The office, like the library, was entirely in keeping with the building, and having reassured her that she didn't mind waiting Hannah sat down in the comfortable armchair the woman had indicated, not opposite the handsome mahogany partners' desk, but in front of the elegant Adam fireplace, opposite a rather larger armchair, which Hannah suspected was the province of Silas Jeffreys himself.

The mouthwatering aroma of coffee filled the room. The secretary had left a tray of it next to her, but Hannah didn't touch it; if anything, she felt even more nervous now than she had done for her first interview.

The door opened, and despite all her training she couldn't prevent herself from turning round. The blood literally left her face, her poise deserting her completely as she stared into the familiar face of the man from the tax office.

'What are you doing here?' she challenged him.

Again she saw the now familiar glint of humour

darken his eyes and curl his mouth.

'It does happen to be my office,' he told her drily.

His office? Hannah couldn't believe it. She looked wildly at him, but something in his eyes beyond the amusement suddenly struck a slight chill through her shock, and even though she couldn't stop herself from saying huskily, 'You're Silas Jeffreys? I don't believe it!' in some odd way she did.

To her utter chagrin she felt a hot tide of betraying colour sweep her skin as he inclined his head in acknowledgement and confirmation.

'But you were working as a tax inspector,' she protested.

He paused for a moment, closed the door, and then came over to her, saying calmly, 'Actually, no, I wasn't. In fact, I'd called at the tax office to pick up my godson. We were having dinner together; he wanted my advice on his career. The receptionist neglected to advise me that he had anyone with him, and when you mistakenly assumed that I was his superior . . . rather than embarrass everyone concerned, I simply went along with your misconception.'

A hundred different thoughts swirled through Hannah's head. She wanted to tell him that he had no right to deceive her, that he could have told her in the library who he was, that surely it was illegal to pose as a tax official when one was no such thing, but, above all that, there was the humiliating and painful knowledge that she had made a complete and utter idiot of herself. For the first time since her early teens, she badly wanted to give vent to her emotions by bursting into tears.

'I apologise if you think I did the wrong thing,' the level male voice continued, making her grit her teeth and blink back the threatening storm, appalled with herself for giving in to such a stupid feminine weakness.

'It was not done with any malice. I had no idea who you were until you left, and by then it was too late. However, I must say one thing, and that is, if you allow those circumstances . . . that incident to prejudice you against taking the post with us, then I shan't try to dissuade you. It isn't often I make a error of judgement, and I don't think I've made one now. Granted, we perhaps haven't had the most advantageous start to our business relationship, but of course it's in your hands whether you choose to accept that what happened was an unfortunate incident and put it in the past, or . . .' He shrugged, and Hannah knew what he was not saying. If she took umbrage, stood up and told him that she was not taking the job, he would let her go, because in doing so she would showing him that she wasn't the kind of person he wanted to employ.

Mirthlessly, Hannah mentally acknowledged his skill in both warning her and complimenting her at the same time.

And, after all, what had he actually done? Nothing . . . not really. An unfortunate chain of circumstances, stemming from one initial mistake. Logically there was no reason why her pride should smart so sorely because she hadn't been possessed with a sixth sense to tell her who he was.

There were a dozen things at least which she ought to have said, but instead she asked him boldly,

'Why was I chosen from all the applicants?'

He looked at her for a moment, and then said firmly, 'Several reasons. Your qualifications were excellent, but then so were those of others. Gordon liked your honesty and openness about your family background. He told me you embraced all the more positive aspects of your sex's rightful liberation, without carrying any of its burdens. I'd given him a brief which specified that I didn't mind which sex my assistant was, just as long as in business conditions they were capable of behaving non-sexually.

'There is no room in this organisation for people who have hang-ups about working with members of the opposite sex,' he added with quiet emphasis. He gave her a thoughtful look, and then added, 'You may as well hear this straight from the horse's mouth, since it's bound to reach you on the grape-vine anyway. My parents were both keen climbers. They were killed in a bad fall when I was seven. My mother's sister, who had just left university, brought me up. She did a correspondence course to qualify as an accountant and then, once she *had* qualified, she worked from home at first, and then from an office in our local market town.

'She sacrificed a great deal to be both mother and provider for me, and it was very, very hard for her. In those days women accountants were few and far between, especially those running their own practices.

'The month after I sat my A levels, she told me she had cancer and that it was inoperable. She'd always wanted to visit Egypt, and so we spent the last three months of her life travelling . . . until she became too ill . . .' He paused, and Hannah found there was an enormous lump in her throat, visualising how hard it must have been both for his aunt as a young girl faced with the task of bringing up and supporting a small child, and then for Silas himself when he knew he was going to lose her.

'When she died, I made myself a promise that I would never differentiate between the mental abilities of men and women. My aunt had proved to me that women are more than equal to men.' He looked at her and said directly, 'Perhaps what I'm trying to tell you is that maybe I was guilty of a small bias towards you because of your sex, but without your own qualifications for the job your sex would not have helped you.'

Hannah understood, and she felt an overwhelming sense of gratitude to that other woman whom she would never meet. How could she allow pride and a sense of having made a fool of herself stand in her way of accepting the job?

'You could have told me who you were when I came for the interview,' she said quietly.

'Yes,' he admitted. 'I hadn't expected anyone to be in the library. I knew you were being interviewed, but I hadn't realised Gordon was running a few minutes late. I thought if I corrected your misapprehension, then it might affect your performance during the interview.'

'I must have seemed very obtuse,' Hannah said ruefully.

'Not obtuse,' he contradicted her, shaking his head. 'A little . . . aggressive, perhaps.' He gave her a smile that took the sting from the words.

'I'd like to accept the job,' she told him.

The expression in his eyes rewarded her decision.

'Good. When can you start?'

Because of holidays due to her but not yet taken, Hannah felt pretty sure she could be free within a fortnight, and told him so.

'That is good. During your first week you'll want to familiarise yourself with my routine and work schedules. As Gordon told you, I try to spend two days a week at least at Padley.'

Hannah gave a small start which he immediately noticed.

'Is something wrong?'

'No. It's just . . . Padley . . . Would that be Padley Court?'

'Yes. Do you know it?'

Hannah nodded. Her mother had mentioned the house to her earlier in the summer, commenting wistfully on the beauty of its garden, which was open to the public on certain days of the year. It was only fifty miles or so from her own home, and she said as much, explaining briefly where her parents lived.

'Yes. Of course. Gordon mentioned to me that your father is a vicar.'

'Yes,' Hannah agreed repressively, not seeing the humour in his smile as she looked away from him. Tilting her chin very firmly, she asked, 'Does my father's calling have any bearing on your job offer?'

'None at all,' he told her gravely, but for once Hannah refused to be appeased. She was still feeling exposed and on edge, after discovering just who he was, and her self-control slipped as she caught the tail end of his smile and burst out crossly, 'And just what is so amusing about my father being a vicar?'

There were still sensitive places in her make-up, left there by the teasing of her peers while she was growing up, some of it kind and some of it cruel. She had been too sensitive in those days. Thankfully she had now learned better . . . or had she, if all it took to set her seething with temper was the mere hint of amusement in silver-grey eyes?

'Nothing,' he told her equably, but his mouth still twitched and he explained drily, 'It's just that somehow I can't quite see you as the dutiful daughter of the manse, visiting the sick with gifts of home-made jam.'

Hannah studied him for a moment, sensing that he was deliberately teasing her, testing her ability to control her emotional reactions to provocation.

'You're rather out of date,' she told him wryly. 'These days the boot is on the other foot, and it's the parishioners who tend to make such donations. Vicars aren't exactly well-paid, and with five children to bring up . . .'

'Five?' His eyebrows lifted, and Hannah repressed the impulse to tell him that he could have read all this on her CV, not realising how skilfully he was drawing her out, gaining her confidence, winning her away from her stance of cool detachment, so that it was easy for him to see the woman beneath the mask of cold professionalism.

'I've got four brothers,' she explained. And as though he could read her mind and see how much those four older and more domineering males had sometimes driven her to despair as she was growing up, and very certainly to resentment as she kicked against their bossiness, he said quietly, 'You're lucky. I envy you. A family is something to be cherished.'

But Hannah wasn't easily convinced.

'If that's what you feel, why are you still single?' she asked him cynically, immediately regretting the words, as she saw too late the trap laid for her by his air of easy camaraderie. This man was her boss, and he would expect some deference to be shown to him, some acknowledgement made of his superiority. She veiled her eyes, cursing her impulsiveness, waiting for him to make some cold and cutting remark about his personal life being his own concern, but to her astonishment he didn't. When the silence had stretched on for so long that she just had to look at him, she saw that he was frowning thoughtfully, as though her question had been one of weighty import.

'The easiest answer would be to say because I haven't yet met the right woman, but that wouldn't strictly be the truth. I have met any number of delightful and eligible women, so I suspect the responsibility for my unmarried state lies within myself. During the years I've been building up the company, any other permanent commitment has been out of the question. The kind of woman who is content to marry, have children and take a back seat in her husband's life is not for me. I want a wife who is my partner in everything I do, who wants to share every single aspect of my life.'

As she listened to him, Hannah felt her stomach give a sudden kick of nervousness, as though suddenly she had stepped into danger. She felt it in the apprehensive sharpening of her senses, the fine lifting of the tiny soft hairs in her nape, the alertness of her body, her muscles tensing so that she trembled slightly inside, outwardly immobile, like a hare catching the scent of the hunter.

'And what about you, Hannah?' he asked her, dexterously altering the axis of their conversation so that it focused on her and not him. 'I know there is no one in your life at the moment, but would you eventually like to marry . . . have a family?'

'No,' she told him shortly, not really sure why she was so quick to give him such an unequivocal denial, why she felt so pressed and endangered, why her senses should leap so convulsively and betrayingly simply because he had closed the gap between them by a few inches as he leaned forward to pick up some papers.

'I intend to dedicate myself fully to my career,' she added in what she had intended to be a firmly dismissive tone, but what, when she heard her own words, sounded fragilely breathless and husky.

He gave her a direct look, his eyes almost silver as they picked up and reflected the light. She wouldn't want to be his antagonist in business or anything else, she acknowledged, while at the same time resenting the knowledge, resenting the purpose and strength she sensed within him, even while she couldn't understand why she should resent them.

'Dedicate? That's a rather strong word to choose. Rather more evocative of a novice about to take her final vows than a modern woman opting for a career.'

He was making a seemingly casual statement, but beneath it lurked a question . . . one that Hannah didn't want to answer. Her facial muscles felt stiff and sore. She was beginning to panic, she acknowledged shakily. She was beginning to feel defensive and vulnerable. She was beginning to adopt all the classic responses of a woman pushed into an inferior position by a man.

Summoning all her strength of will, she managed to force herself to relax and smile, even though doing so made her feel as though her tense flesh was splitting.

'Perhaps dedicate was the wrong word to use,' she allowed. 'But certainly my career is the main focus of my life.'

'And if that changed . . . if you met someone and found that he was more important to you . . .'

Once again panic attacked her; a familiar panic this time, the one she always experienced whenever she thought of committing herself completely to another human being. But this was a panic she was used to . . . one which she could and did control.

'That won't happen,' she told him with calm assurance, lifting her eyes to his face, and surprising there a look of such curious concentration that it was seconds before she could bring herself to look away, and then only because someone knocked hesitantly on the door.

'That will be my secretary. I have a board meeting in fifteen minutes. We'll be in touch with you regarding everything we've discussed today.'

He got up and stretched out his hand, and Hannah

followed suit. His skin felt cool and firm against her own, the faint callouses on his palms abrasive against her skin, their presence surprising her into a faint frown, as she wondered how he had got them. Certainly not running the Jeffreys Group.

CHAPTER FOUR

ON AN impulse even she herself couldn't entirely understand, Hannah decided to go home for the weekend.

Her mother sounded surprised, but pleased when Hannah rang to ask her if it would be all right, quickly assuring her that they would be delighted to see her.

'Matt will be home as well,' her mother informed her. Matt, a highly qualified mineral engineer, had set up in business as a consultant six months ago, and the business was doing very well, but kept him extremely busy. 'He's bringing a friend with him. They're both en route for Australia.

'He used to work with Matt, apparently, and since they're travelling to Australia together and only here for a couple of days, Matt asked if it would be all right if he brought him home with him.'

Matt and one of his mining engineer colleagues . . . Hannah pulled a face into the receiver, but it was too late to change her mind now. Her mother would be hurt. As she replaced it, Hannah grimaced ruefully to herself. Matt would no doubt spend the entire weekend teasing her, and his Australian colleague would probably follow suit. In her older brothers' eyes, she would never be allowed to grow up. She would always remain their little sister, and she would always have to suffer their good-natured but sometimes irritating teasing. It was no wonder none of them was married yet, she reflected darkly as she packed her weekend bag. Her mother had spoiled them and they were too chauvinistic. Their chosen careers in fields which were almost entirely masculine didn't help, either.

A couple of hours later, as she drove homewards, she decided that she would keep the good news about her company car until she and her parents were alone. She wondered what time Matt would be arriving; not until she herself was settled in, she hoped. She loved her brothers, but she would have appreciated having her parents to herself for the weekend.

As she turned into the vicarage drive and saw the hire car parked there, she realised that she was out of luck. It was too late now to wish that she had not already told her parents about her new job. They would want to talk about it, and she was not sure she wanted to go into all the details in front of a stranger.

Although the vicarage possessed a very handsome, if somewhat shabby Georgian front door, no one used it; partly because the bell didn't work, and partly because the majority of his parishioners knew that her father's study overlooked the rear of the garden and was closer to the back door.

This being the case, Hannah was astounded to see the front door opening as she got out of her car and retrieved her weekend case from the boot.

As the door opened, she saw two men standing in the hallway, deep in conversation. One of them was Matt, her brother, and the other obviously his colleague.

Neither of them had noticed her arrival, and so Hannah was at liberty to study them. It was over twelve months since she had last seen her brother, but he hadn't changed, apart from a deepening in the richness of his tan. His companion lacked Matt's lean height, but was just as broad-shouldered and burned by the sun. He saw her first, his eyes widening a little as he looked at her, his male appreciation of her in direct contrast to her brother's casual, 'Oh, there you are, brat. Malcolm here reckons he can fix the bell. Malcolm, meet my kid sister.' He saw Hannah's glower and grinned at her.

'Sorry, brat,' he added affectionately. 'I tend to forget you're a real high-flyer these days. Got yourself a new job, I hear . . . working for Silas Jeffreys.'

'That's right,' Hannah agreed calmly, refusing to respond to the bait being laid so tantalisingly and so obviously, turning from her brother to his colleague and saying quietly, 'I doubt if you'll be able to do much with the bell. It's original, you see, and some of the parts——'

'If anyone can fix it, Malc can,' Matt interrupted her. 'He's a whiz with anything electrical. If you've got anything you need plugs putting on . . .' He grinned infuriatingly at her while Hannah suppressed the urge to stick her tongue out at him. It was still very much an 'in' joke among her brothers how, as a very young teenager, and determined to show them that there was nothing they could do that she could not, she had wired up a plug for her new hairdryer wrongly, and had consequently fused every plug socket in the vicarage.

She had learned better since then, but they refused to let the old story die. Giving Matt an exasperated glance, she smiled at Malcolm and walked past them both into the kitchen.

Her mother welcomed her fondly, insisting that she sit down while she made her a cup of tea.

'I won't ask you about your job yet. You can tell us all about it over dinner. Isn't it marvellous, Matt being home? And Malcolm is so nice . . .'

Recognising the matchmaking glint in her mother's eyes, Hannah hastily announced that she ought to unpack, sidetracking her mother by offering cleverly to help pick the last of the soft fruit, and asking so many questions about the garden that there was no room in the conversation for Malcolm.

'Oh, you'll never guess what . . .' she added, on the point of leaving the kitchen. 'Silas Jeffreys, my new boss, is the owner of Padley Court. Apparently he spends a certain portion of each week working from the Court. I don't know how much free time I'll have while we're there . . . not much at first, I don't suppose, but perhaps later when I'm more on top of the job, I might be able to pop over in the evening.'

'Padley Court? Surely he isn't living there?' her mother interrupted, frowning at her. 'From what I've heard the house is practically derelict. Lord and Lady Padley were only living in a handful of the rooms you know. Every penny they had to spare went on the garden. And when Lady Padley died——' She broke off as the telephone rang, and Hannah made her escape.

Her room was on the third floor of the vicarage. As children, all of them had had these attic rooms with their sloping ceilings and small windows, and then, as the boys graduated to the larger second-floor rooms, Hannah had found that she enjoyed the privacy of having the entire third floor to herself and so she had retained her childhood bedroom.

Her bedroom had a small window-seat, barely large enough for her now, but still one of her favourite places. From the window she could see for miles, right across to the purple blue line of hills in the distance. The room got the evening sun, mellowing and softening the unevenness of the plastered walls and their faded wallpaper, picking out motes of dust that danced on the air, warming the room with the scent of the old-fashioned Bourbon rose that climbed the wall outside.

As she watched, she saw a fox streak across the field beyond the house and heard the harsh cry of a pair of geese winging their way overhead. There was a wildfowl sanctuary not many miles away, not entirely popular with all the local residents, who claimed that the herons decimated the populations of their fishponds.

She saw her father arrive home and climb stiffly out of his car. Matt came out of the house and clapped a hand on his shoulder, and she stifled a small sigh. Their father was tall, as tall as the boys, but now Matt seemed the taller, their father stooped and stiff. Soon she would have to go down and help her mother with the evening meal, and Matt, watching her, would give her that wicked smile of his. How they had fought as children, as she had demanded equal treatment to her brothers, as she had insisted, backed up by her father, that her chores were theirs.

It had worked both ways, though. In the winter one of the boys' tasks had been to clear the snow and ice away from the vicarage driveway, and she had had to do her part. Equal treatment all round, but that hadn't stopped the boys burying her in the snow and pretending she was a snowman; nor her retaliating by making tiny holes in all their hot-water bottles, not discovered until they were filled and in bed. She laughed reluctantly to herself, acknowledging that there had been occasions when she had played shamelessly upon her sex to get her own back on them.

Changing into jeans and a sweatshirt, she went downstairs and into the kitchen, coming to a full stop when she saw that her mother wasn't alone, and that Malcolm was with her, apparently peeling potatoes.

He gave her a friendly smile and said, 'I was just telling your mother that when I was a kid this was always my job, and with three big sisters to make sure I stuck at it . . .'

'Three sisters . . . did they bully you as much as my brothers bullied me?' Hannah asked him feelingly.

He laughed and agreed that they had, and within minutes they were exchanging lurid stories of their childhoods, talking together as though they had known one another for years.

Long before they sat down for dinner she discovered that he was a highly trained electrical engineer who had worked alongside her brother in the research and development side of the mining industry, and over dinner he kept them all entertained with amusing stories of his experiences.

Afterwards, while he and Matt washed up, Hannah made the coffee, and then later, relaxed and seated in front of the sitting-room fire, she allowed herself to be drawn out about her own career and her new job.

'Silas Jeffreys. That's really high-flying,' Matt commented. 'You've done well there, kid. What did you do? Flash those long legs of yours at him?'

He was only teasing her, Hannah knew, controlling her indignant response mock sweetly. 'No such thing. Is that how you got that job at MacDonalds, before you decided to go it alone, brother dear?'

Malcolm almost choked on his coffee, while to her astonishment Hannah realised that Matt was actually embarrassed.

'She's got you there.' Malcolm grinned at him, and then, turning to Hannah, explained, 'MacDonalds was a family-owned company, and the owner had an extremely beautiful daughter whom he was training to take over from him . . . What *did* you do when you went for your interview, Matt?' he asked wickedly. 'Tear open your shirt and——'

'Cut it out . . .' Matt moved uncomfortably in his chair.

And it was left to their father to diplomatically turn the conversation into less explosive channels.

It was late when Hannah eventually went to bed. Malcolm was a good conversationalist . . . He had worked all over the world, and had a fund of stories to relate, and Hannah hadn't realised how late it was until she'd started yawning.

Having three extra people to cater for could only add to her mother's already heavy workload, and she intended to be up early in the morning to help her.

As always when she was at home, she fell asleep almost the moment her head touched the pillow, waking up abruptly just after six o'clock with vivid memories of a dream which had somehow featured Silas Jeffreys, and which had been confusingly set in one of the locations Malcolm had described to them last night. In her dream it had been her task to put right a piece of electrical equipment of unbelievable complexity, and although she had not even known where to start, when Silas had suddenly materialised beside her and offered to do it for her she had refused his help stubbornly, insisting on working on her own until her fingers grew so clumsy that she had pushed the whole thing away from her. He had come and crouched down beside her then, carefully showing her what had to be done, placing his hands over hers as he directed her fingers. She clenched and unclenched them now, disturbed to discover that they were actually tingling, as though that contact had been real.

Not wanting to dwell on the dream, she got up, showering and then getting dressed. Her mother was always up for seven, but for once she could have a small lie-in and a cup of tea, Hannah decided, making her way downstairs, only to find that the kitchen wasn't empty as she had expected. Malcolm was already standing in front of the boiling kettle.

He apologised when he saw her, explaining that he was used to rising early. 'I'd thought of walking into the village and getting a paper, but I wasn't sure what time the shops opened.'

'The post office will be open,' Hannah confirmed, nodding as he asked if she wanted tea. He was a nice man . . . pleasant, intelligent . . . and she sensed that with very little effort at all she could draw him to her, but instinctively she knew she wouldn't. She liked him, but nothing more, and it bolstered her badly dented confidence to be confronted with such an eligible and charming man and to know that he represented no threat whatsoever to her career.

That tiny moment of self-doubt in Silas's office was totally unimportant, an irrational reaction to the strain of attending the interview, an odd kick-up in her normal responses, something she could quite confidently forget and put behind her.

The weekend passed very quickly. On Saturday night, at Hannah's suggestion, the three of them went out for a meal.

On Sunday she attended morning communion. Once they were into their teens her father had never forced his faith on to any of his children, but every now and again Hannah enjoyed the experience of the simple ritual with its cleansing, healing benedictions.

She met Matt and Malcolm on the way back, and agreed to go with them for a drink. They had just reached the village when a car drew up in front of them at the pedestrian crossing. Hannah recognised the Daimler saloon instantly, her startled glance darting from its familiar paintwork to its even more familiar driver.

'Silas!' Her heart gave a floundering leap of shocked recognition as she said his name.

He was looking straight at her, and she was

oblivious to Matt's frowning look of query, or the protective weight of Malcolm's arm around her waist as he prevented her from stepping off the pavement.

There was a woman seated next to Silas. A woman whose beauty and elegance made Hannah wonder who she was. She moved slightly, placing one hand on Silas's arm and saying something to him, and then, after another lightning dissecting glance that seemed to linger deliberately on her waist, where Malcolm's hand rested, Silas looked away and the car moved on.

'Who was that?' Matt demanded.

'My new boss.'

'Mm. His wife looks expensive.'

'She isn't his wife. He isn't married,' Hannah told him shortly.

The pub was busy, but despite the pleasant atmosphere and the conversation Hannah found it impossible to recapture her earlier relaxed mood.

She blamed its loss on the unexpected appearance of Silas Jeffreys, bound no doubt for Padley Court. Had he spent the weekend there with *her*? Hannah could feel a hot flush staining her skin. What business of hers was it where he spent his weekends, or with whom? What was wrong with her, for goodness' sake? She was pretty sure that the unexpected sight of her present boss with an unknown woman at his side wouldn't have affected her like this.

Uneasily she wondered if taking this job was a wise thing to do. If she was brutally honest with herself, and she knew she was going to have to be, she found Silas very attractive. Even at the most basic physical level, her body had reacted to him when she didn't know him, and now the discovery that that powerful physical presence belonged to a man whose intelligence and shrewdness she had long admired was making a mockery of her fiercely held determination to remain immune to the vulnerabilities of her sex.

She couldn't *afford* to be attracted to him, she told herself helplessly later in the afternoon, brooding over the slyness of fate. Had it been any other man who affected her like this, she would have been relatively safe. She could simply have cut him out of her life, now, at the start, before . . . Before what? she asked herself, drawing up her knees and hugging her arms round them as she sat in the shadowy corner of the garden on the lawn. She was supposed to be picking blackberries. She looked down at her basket. It was almost half-full. Grimacing, she unclasped her knees and got up reluctantly. The trouble with such a mechanical task was that it left her with too much time to think, to worry. But what was there to worry about? Surely she didn't doubt her own ability to control that hitherto dormant, feminine side of her nature which was telling her so plainly that it found Silas attractive? As she wandered restlessly into the field and along the hedge, automatically picking the fruit off the thorny branches, she acknowledged that she wanted the challenge of her new job too much to listen to any voice of caution.

She had just made a major life-enhancing decision . . . it was only natural that she should react to that by experiencing a certain amount of stress, and it was well-known that stress did odd things to people, made them react in peculiar ways. That was all there was to this unsettling, unfamiliar sensation that prickled across her skin and tightened her muscles whenever she thought about or saw Silas. It was simply a manifestation of stress. Yes, that was definitely it. She was merely suffering from stress. Once she had settled into her new job, everything would be all right.

She left for London later that evening, nodding vaguely when Matt said something about possibly staying overnight with her later in the year on his way to a technical conference in Amsterdam, without really paying much attention to what he was saying. She simply said her goodbyes and climbed into her car.

Just over a fortnight later, at eight o'clock on a Monday morning, her stomach alive with the butterflies beating frantic wings inside it, she was stepping inside the offices of the Jeffreys Group, this time not as an interviewee but as a member of its staff.

Her new company car had been delivered to her on Friday evening. Her father's pleasure at finding himself the owner of her Volvo had made her realise anew how difficult financially things were for her parents. And yet they were happy, enviably so, because they had learned the secret of being content. Would she ever find such contentment? Did she even want to? She dismissed the restless nervous sensation afflicting her, and with outward calmness gave her name to the receptionist.

The girl responded with a warm, natural smile.

'Of course. Mr Jeffreys said to expect you. If you go upstairs in the lift, his secretary will be waiting for you. She'll show you where your office is and familiarise you with the layout of the building.'

Silas's secretary greeted her with a smile as warm as the receptionist's, which pleased Hannah. It was plain that this elegant, efficient woman harboured no resentment against other successful members of her own sex; not an uncommon occurrence, as Hannah had discovered.

'Your office is next to Silas's,' the older woman told her, escorting her towards it. 'There's an inter-connecting door, and of course I'll make sure your secretary has a full copy of his diary appointments, so that you needn't worry about walking in on him when he's in a meeting, although I should imagine that, as his assistant, he'll want you to join him for most of his appointments.

'This week things aren't too hectic. He's booked down Thursday and Friday as his days at Padley, and he did say to mention to you that if you wished you needn't come back to town on Friday, but to stay on and visit your parents—that was fine by him.' She gave Hannah a warm smile. 'I understand your family live near Padley. I envy you. It's such a beautiful part of the world.'

A little to her own surprise, Hannah found herself unbending enough to say, 'Yes. My father is the vicar of a relatively small market town, more of a large village, really——'

She broke off as the older woman opened the door into what was Hannah's office. Not much smaller than Silas's, it was furnished with similar attention to detail. Her eye was caught by two blue and white patterned jugs standing on the hearth of the room's fireplace. They were filled with fresh, cottagy flowers, and as she saw Hannah looking at them Margaret Bannerman said easily, 'Silas asked me to organise them. He's marvellous about things like that. There's no sexual discrimination at all within the Jeffreys Group, but neither does he expect us to be token men. All the girls get an extra hour off one day a week so that they can get their hair done. Silas never employs a woman because of the way she looks, but he does expect all his staff to present a smart appearance.'

'No need to ask if you like working for him,' Hannah commented, not sure if she really approved of such a potentially paternalistic and therefore vaguely Victorian attitude in an employer.

'Like it?' Margaret grinned at her. 'It's the best job I've ever had. Hard work, of course. Silas isn't exactly a workaholic, but my goodness, he knows how to pack sixty very full seconds into every working minute. It's his consideration for others, though, that makes him so marvellous to work for. He's no soft touch, but he's always ready to listen, and he's appreciative of the effort everyone puts in. And not just financially . . .'

Hannah was tempted to point out to her that what she termed 'consideration' could perhaps be simply good business strategy. After all, it was well-known that a workforce worked more efficiently and profitably when it was treated well. But she subdued the words. There was no point in antagonising the other woman, and Hannah sensed that any criticism of her boss *would* be taken as antagonism.

'Silas should be arriving any minute. He told me to tell you that he'd brief you himself once he gets in. Just give him half an hour to go through the post.'

There was a small office off Hannah's, and as they were talking the door into it opened and a pretty, dark-haired girl walked in, looking around uncertainly.

'Ah, Sarah,' Margaret called out. 'Come in and I'll introduce you. Sarah will be your secretary,' Margaret told her, introducing the dark-haired girl to Hannah, and then with another smile she excused herself and headed back to her own office.

In the next fifteen minutes, Hannah learned that Sarah had been with the company just over six months. She took to the younger girl instantly, liking her friendly, helpful manner and sensing that she was a girl who would work hard.

She also learned that Gordon Giles, who had initially interviewed her, was presently away in the States on business, and for some reason that made her feel rather nervous, although she had no idea what she was feeling nervous about.

No idea, that was, until Sarah had left her to go and get them both some coffee and the communicating door between her own office and Silas's opened and he walked in, giving her a courteous good morning.

He was wearing a dark suit this morning with an immaculate white shirt and a striped tie. He looked at her shrewdly as she stood tensely beside her desk, and said calmingly, 'Don't worry. You're bound to feel a few tremors of apprehension for a few days. Everyone does when they first take on a new job.

I expect Maggie's already told you that I'd like to run over a few things with you after I've checked through the post. Just come through to my office at, say, half-past nine.'

He gave Sarah a friendly smile as she came in carrying the coffee, and after he had gone Hannah tried to steady her pounding heart, telling herself that she was behaving like a fool.

She had dressed carefully this morning in one of her severe businesslike suits and a crisp white shirt. The starched collar was rubbing slightly against her neck, and she looked enviously at Sarah's pretty silk dress.

Female executives did not wear silk.

It was too soft, too womanly. It conveyed images in direct opposition to those a woman executive wished to convey. Her tailored suit was far more in keeping with the image she liked to project, and yet . . . and yet . . . Something almost approaching a faintly regretful sigh built up inside her. It must be the office having this odd effect on her. Yes, that was it, she reflected in relief. It was the office, with its Georgian elegance, its soft colour-washed walls and the richness of the rug on the polished floor. A rug which she was uneasily aware looked far too rich and old to be a mere copy of the original Savonière, as she had at first assumed it must be.

A boss who provided his employees with offices furnished with priceless antiques, who treated his female employees as individuals and cherished them for the very difference in their sex to his own . . . Hannah decided that it must be her hardy upbringing that made her feel so uncomfortable and faintly suspicious. The simple truth was that she wasn't used to such luxury and comfort in the workplace.

But she was going to have to accustom herself to it, and to an environment where it was no longer necessary for her to rigorously monitor her every instinctive response lest some male colleague jeer at it as an unwanted 'feminine' reaction.

Here, it seemed, feminine reactions were welcomed for the insight they gave into human relationships and vulnerabilities. A brief tap on her door disturbed her chain of thought.

'It's half-past nine,' Sarah told her shyly.

CHAPTER SIX

'HANNAH, good! Come in and sit down . . .'

Silas had been seated behind his desk when she walked in, but now he stood up, beckoning her to join him in the more informal seating arrangement around the fire.

His small courtesy on standing as she entered threw her for a moment, and she realised as she felt herself stiffening defensively how very prickly she must have become during the last extremely difficult months of working with Brian Howard.

'Maggie will be giving Sarah a list of our major current clients. I've got a copy here, and one of the first things I want to do is to run through it with you. We're in the business of selling here, not always an easy task, and sometimes we find we get a client who is particularly difficult to deal with. If you have any problems with any of the clients, please tell me——'

He was frowning slightly, and Hannah bristled instinctively, cutting across what he was saying to demand, 'If you felt I might have trouble handling your clients, why did you offer me the job?'

'You were employed as vice-president and as my personal assistant,' he reminded her. 'But as a matter of fact that advice was for your benefit and not theirs. It sometimes happens that a businessman will expect to be provided with extra-curricular activities of a kind which we do not and never will supply. All the women who work for me have explicit instructions to report such men to their superiors. The Jeffreys Group does not do business with them again,' he told her crisply.

As she looked away from him, angry with herself for leaping to a totally erroneous conclusion, and taking personally something which had obviously merely been meant as a general warning, she heard him saying, 'I take it you enjoyed your weekend at home?'

Her heart leapt. So he *had* seen her.

'Very much,' she responded neutrally, wondering whether she was expected to ask him if he had enjoyed his, and reflecting a little sourly that he could surely not have failed to do so with such a stunningly attractive female companion.

After a moment's silence, Hannah looked at him and found him watching her with an expression she found it hard to define.

'Maggie has told you, presumably, that we shall be spending Thursday and Friday at Padley?'

'Yes,' Hannah agreed formally.

Again he looked at her, a cool, assessing look that didn't linger on her face, but went directly instead to her clothes . . . and stayed there for so long that Hannah found she was holding her breath, her heart pumping fiercely. What was he looking at her for? His scrutiny unnerved her, made her feel vulnerable and awkward. Her mouth went dry and she found herself swallowing nervously. The movement of her throat muscles attracted his attention, and he switched his concentration from her clothes to her skin, making an odd heat that generated from the pit of her stomach and which weakened every muscle in her body, climbed swiftly through her veins and turned her skin a faint pink.

She swallowed again, totally unable to help herself, wondering if she was trembling visibly as much as she was trembling inwardly.

She waited, hardly daring to breathe, knowing that Silas must be aware of her tension, waiting for him to ask her what was wrong, but instead he merely said levelly, 'Power dressing has its place in the modern business world, but it isn't necessary here. Of course, I don't want to dictate to any member of my staff how they should dress. But it occurs to me on those occasions when we visit Padley that you might want to wear something a little more casual, rather more comfortable.'

Hannah had always been vulnerable to criticism. It was a weakness she had striven all her life to hide, but now for some reason her defences deserted her, and she reacted quickly and bitterly to Silas's words, pain stinging her over-sensitive emotions as she retaliated sharply, 'How very typical of a man. I suppose you'd prefer me to wear something like the dress Sarah has on . . . something soft and feminine with tactile appeal . . .'

As he started to frown, she realised too late what she had done. For all his apparent indulgence, this man was her boss. She should never have allowed him to push her into such a personal exchange.

And then, just as she was formulating a stiff apology, his frown vanished and his mouth twitched in a faint smile.

'Attractive though it is, Sarah's outfit isn't exactly what I had in mind. Cyclamen pink is hardly your colour, I suspect,' he added drily, and then, before she could object to the blatant chauvinism of his remarks, he continued smoothly, 'I have a luncheon engagement today with an old client. I've arranged for you to join us. Although initially you won't have much contact with the clients, later on when you've found your feet, so to speak, there may be occasions when I shall ask you to stand in for me. We're lunching at . . .'

He mentioned a restaurant which Hannah well knew was one of the most fashionable and expensive in the City. She also knew that her City suit would look totally out of place among the designer outfits of the other female diners, and she groaned mentally.

In the event, the lunch was not the ordeal Hannah had anticipated. They arrived at the restaurant ahead of the client, who when he joined them proved to be a pleasant man in his early thirties; his manner was perhaps a little too smooth and polished for Hannah's taste, but he was careful to keep her fully involved in the conversation, doing nothing more than raising his eyebrows slightly when Silas introduced her as his personal assistant.

From the conversation, Hannah soon realised that Silas had apparently embarked on something of a crusade in involving as many women as he could in his business; and that this crusade was well-known among his friends and clients.

The lunch was not a selling exercise, but simply an affirmation of the good relationship that already obviously existed with the client, and afterwards, as they left the restaurant, Hannah felt relaxed enough to ask Silas several questions about Tim Hawley and his business.

Indeed, so engrossed was she that she stepped off the pavement without thinking, gasping out loud when Silas's arm shot out and he grabbed hold of her, swinging her back, just as a taxi screamed round the corner far too fast.

Shaken and angry with herself, Hannah thanked him. All her life her family had teased her for being impetuous and slightly clumsy, and she didn't like having their teasing confirmed by the knowledge that but for Silas's awareness and prompt action she might have been injured by the taxi.

As the immediate shock passed, she realised that Silas was still holding her, his hand gripping her arm so tightly that she could feel pins and needles under her skin. She must have made a faint sound of distress without realising it, because immediately his grip relaxed, although he didn't release her. It was odd how aware she was of the heat and strength of his flesh, even through the thickness of her jacket. Her skin seemed to burn from the contact, a fierce, consuming heat that sent pulses of energy singing through her body. An unfamiliar faintness came over her, a combination of shock and anger, she told herself, as she tried to control it and the horrid buzzing in her ears. She concentrated on focusing on Silas's face. His skin looked rather pale, the hard jut of his cheekbones uncompromisingly male. Through her dizziness, she felt a dangerous compulsion to reach out and touch them with her fingers.

Abruptly, despite the heat he was generating in her body, she started to shiver. She watched distantly and vaguely as his eyebrows contracted and he frowned at her, feeling his fingers splay out against her arm and his other hand reach for her wrist, cool fingers monitoring her frantic pulse. He said something under his breath, extinguished by the roar of the traffic as the light changed.

'Hannah.' He shook her, and she realised that the look in his eyes was one of concern. Why—because he had registered that all too betraying and very feminine reaction to him? The thought made her go hot again with chagrin and despair. This was the very situation she had been determined to avoid.

Gathering her stunned wits, she pulled away from him, apologising huskily for her clumsiness. Before she looked away from him, she saw his frown deepen and her heart sank. Was he already regretting employing her? Fraught with difficulties though her new job was, she didn't want to lose it.

And then, to her astonishment, she heard him say tersely, 'You weren't clumsy; the taxi driver was at fault . . .' Far more roughly he added, 'He could have killed you. Another few inches . . .'

Her face went ashen as she looked at him and the reality of what he was saying hit her in all its starkness. She could so easily have been killed. A moment's lack of concentration, a moment's unawareness . . . and then oblivion. A shudder of horror convulsed her. She felt sick and dizzy, hot and then dangerously, weakeningly cold. Shock, she told herself inwardly, her body registering the presence of Silas's arm around her with gratitude for its warmth and comfort, instincts she had long ago thought successfully suppressed, surging past the barriers of training and life-style as she allowed herself to draw strength from his proximity, leaning gratefully against him while the waves of sickness and dizziness washed over her and the roaring in her ears subsided to no more than the wash of conversation of people walking past them; some of them staring at them, others totally uninterested in their stillness . . . in the proximity of their bodies that was almost but not quite an embrace.

The realisation of what she was doing brought Hannah abruptly out of Silas's arms. She heard him saying something about it being his fault, and that he shouldn't have frightened her by highlighting her danger.

She managed to pull herself together sufficiently to give him a weak smile and say shakily, 'I'm only grateful I wasn't with one of my brothers. They're always reminding me how impulsive and careless I am.'

'I take it those were two of your brothers I saw you with on Sunday?' Silas asked her as they crossed the road in safety and continued to make their way back to the office.

Without looking at him, Hannah shook her head. 'One of them was. The other was a . . . a friend——'

Of my brother's, she had been about to add, but to her astonishment Silas cut right across what she was telling him to say crisply, and with a certain amount of coldness, 'There's no need to be coy, Hannah. If the man is your lover, then why not say so?'

'If he was, I would,' Hannah asserted a little

untruthfully. 'As it happens, Malcolm and I had only met this weekend. He's a colleague of my brother's.'

The dark eyebrows rose.

'Really? You surprise me. I had surmised from the very possessive way he was holding on to you that the relationship between the two of you was far more intimate.'

'Even if it were, that would scarcely be any business of yours,' Hannah told him, jolted out of her habitual caution by the note of interrogation she could detect in his voice.

'On the contrary. When you were interviewed for your job, you informed Gordon that your life was completely free of any emotional commitments.'

Thoroughly angry now, Hannah stopped on the pavement and challenged him. 'And you thought I was lying? Well, I wasn't,' she told him flatly, too angry to employ tact. 'There *is* no man in my life . . . no lover to whom I'm committed. Not now, not in the past, and not in the future.'

She stopped, aware of a brief flaring of something disconcerting in his eyes, before he banished it and said smoothly, 'I'm very tempted to ask you what it is about the male sex that makes you so determined to exclude them from your life, but now isn't the time.'

They were almost back at the office, and too late Hannah realised she had allowed herself to become involved in a far more personal discussion than was wise . . . or safe.

Safe. There it was again, that word that Linda had said was so favoured by their generation. She tensed a little uncomfortably, remembering the sensation that had raced through her when Silas had touched her. Sensations which had been far from safe . . .

'I've got a board meeting this afternoon. I'd like you to sit in on it. Tomorrow I'll want your reaction and appraisal of the other board members, then we'll go through the facts about them and see just how keen your judgement is.'

He was testing her, but at least he was giving her fair warning. Normally Hannah considered herself to be a pretty fair judge of character, but today she had been thrown so off guard by her own emotional and physical vulnerability that her confidence seemed to be draining away from her like life blood from a major artery. She gave Silas a suspicious glance, wondering whether he had done it on purpose, just to see exactly how she would cope. He was a very shrewd man, very skilled at manipulating people, no matter how sincere he might appear on the surface.

She was just about to step past him into the building when he said abruptly, 'Wait.'

As she turned towards him in mute query, he reached out and cupped her face in his hands.

Instantly, all her bones liquefied. Her stomach became a trembling mass of jelly, and where his hands touched her skin, holding her face as though it were made of the most fragile porcelain, her skin seemed to burn.

She thought he was actually going to kiss her, and stared at him in confused bewilderment, wondering which of them had gone mad.

How could he possibly know of the appallingly intense desire inside her to know what his kiss would be like? How could he read her so clearly that he could turn to her so prosaically and matter-of-factly, here on the pavement outside his offices and place his mouth to hers? Like an adult giving sweets to a child. Shamingly, the fear grew that somehow she herself had told him, had shown him, had asked him . . . There could be no other explanation for the ease and assurance with which he had stopped her, with which he was holding her.

And yet she would have sworn that, of all men, he was the least likely to indulge in such behaviour with an employee.

She felt both triumph and disappointment: triumph that he should so immediately respond to her femininity, and disappointment at his lack of control, of responsibility.

As her thoughts swirled fiercely through her mind, he removed one hand from her face and said calmly, 'You've got a smut on your cheekbone. It doesn't go with the power dressing. I'd go and check up on it before going back to your desk if I were you. It doesn't match the image.'

And then he was releasing her, smiling at her in a kindly, distant manner, while she could only stand transfixed and stare at him, so thoroughly confused and betrayed by her own emotions that speech was literally impossible.

Later in the afternoon, sitting in on the board meeting, she refused to allow herself to berate herself any longer. All right, so she had come dangerously close to making a fool of herself. Well, let that be a lesson to her. She frowned fiercely, trying to concentrate on what was going on.

The board wasn't excessively large. Under a

dozen members, most of their names familiar to her from her pre-interview research; mostly but not all of them involved with the Group in one capacity or another, all of them very able and shrewd businessmen. All of them, under the eagle scrutiny of Silas's eyes, treating her as an equal.

It was almost six o'clock before the meeting finished. One of the directors suggested they all went on to a local pub for a drink, and Hannah's heart sank. She felt wrung out both emotionally and physically, and had planned to spend the evening going over some of the client files.

She didn't allow her feelings to show, however, waiting for Silas's response to the other director's suggestion.

To her relief he vetoed it, explaining that he had a dinner engagement. With the woman she had seen with him in his car? Hannah wondered, and then fought to dismiss her dangerous train of thought, concentrating instead on the final winding up of the meeting.

Knowing that her first few days in her new environment would be physically and mentally punishing, she had deliberately kept this evening free, but it seemed that fate was determined to conspire against her, and, by the time she had finished assuring her mother that she loved her new job, it was gone nine o'clock and her stomach was reminding her that she hadn't eaten since lunchtime.

Half an hour later, shoes off, feet tucked up underneath her, she was sitting in her favourite chair with a bowl of crisp raw vegetables on the table beside her, deeply engrossed in the files she was studying, when the phone rang again.

Cursing mildly, she got up to answer it. Linda was on the other end of the line, wanting to talk about her weekend. Listening to Linda extolling her lover's virtues, her heart sank a little. She wanted to caution her friend against allowing herself to become too emotionally involved, but just as she opened her mouth to do so she had a vivid memory of her own feelings this afternoon when Silas had touched her, and the caution died unspoken. Who was she to give advice? She was already in dire danger of committing the greatest folly known to a female employee . . . that of falling in love with her boss.

Falling in love . . . She moved restlessly on her chair, no longer really listening to her friend, conscious of the growing schism within her own personality. More and more often now, the softer, more traditional, more emotional and vulnerable side of her nature broke through her self-imposed banishment of it. It was no use blaming Silas. He was simply the focus of those emotions, not the cause.

She heard Linda saying goodbye and responded automatically; her desire to work had gone. She wandered restlessly round her apartment, finally picking up a magazine which she had bought on impulse over the weekend and then discarded.

There was an article in it on women who opted for motherhood in their late thirties; career women who without exception were extolling the virtues of motherhood.

Hannah looked at the photographs with a tiny

shudder, acknowledging an inherent fear of studying them too closely.

Why? Because she was afraid that the opinions and emotions of those women featured in the article might be contagious? The she might become a victim of the baby fever that had gripped them? That she might—appalling thought—experience that same urge to succumb to the siren call of nature?

Impossible, she told herself, throwing the magazine aside, irritated with herself for the dangerous game she was almost deliberately playing with her own emotions and vulnerabilities. It was rather like the game of 'chicken' she had played at school as a child. Only now she was her own rival.

Despite all her good intentions, it was late when she went to bed, and for once the rhythmic sound of the river did not lull her to sleep.

Like some uncontrollable sickness she couldn't withstand, she started to think about Silas . . . to wonder what he was doing, who he was with. She remembered how she had felt when he had touched her, and shuddered deeply, completely unaware of the low moan that rose in her throat, trying not to visualise him with *her* . . . the *soignée* woman she had seen him with in his car. She was berating herself . . . hating herself for what she was doing, both to herself and, by virtue of the intrusiveness of her thoughts into his personal life, to him.

The week passed all too quickly. Her work proved challenging, almost exhaustingly so, for which Hannah was grateful. Deep down inside her a small voice still warned her that she was in danger, that she ought not to have taken the job, but she ignored it, subduing both it and her emotions by relentlessly refusing to acknowledge their existence.

Faces and names became familiar to her, the hierarchy of the Group more clear, the names of its clients coming automatically to her lips instead of having to be memorised.

She was delighted to see how much Silas was prepared to delegate work to her and how much responsibility she would have. In fact, were it not for her unwanted awareness of Silas as man, rather than as an astute financier, she would have been able to describe her life as not far short of perfect.

A longstanding dinner engagement on Wednesday evening, with an old group of friends she had known for many years, gave her the opportunity to announce her career move.

All of them were openly envious, congratulating her on her good luck. All of them took their careers seriously, and none of them questioned her on her reaction to Silas on a personal level, but, instead of feeling relief, she felt rather a fraud . . . as though the division within her own nature was already in some subtle way separating her from these serious, dedicated young women; it was as though her very hormones were making her a traitor to the ideals she had held for so long, and the appalling thing was that she didn't seem to be able to do a thing about it. No matter how strict a control she kept over herself during her waking hours, at night while she was asleep her dreams became turbulent and erotic, stirring up sensations that lingered even while she was awake, giving her an insight into her own nature she would rather not have had.

Desire . . . sexual chemistry . . . give it what name you would, the havoc that such an awareness could bring made her shudder in dread, but she had it under control, she assured herself later in the evening as she drove home. She was already packed for the overnight stay at Padley Court, and she had warned her parents to expect her home for the weekend. Her motives in going home were complex and not without a certain deviousness. Given the busy pace of her mother's life, she was bound to be kept far too busy to dwell on Silas and her reaction to him.

Every now and again the cold voice of reason told her that it would be safer to simply give up her job, but she couldn't bear to do it. She loved the challenges of her work. She loved the scope and encouragement Silas gave her. She loved the atmosphere that permeated the entire Jeffreys organisation, right from its most junior member of staff, and she knew that there was much she could learn from Silas.

As she stopped the car she had an electrifying, undermining mental vision of him reaching out to touch her, his lean hands caressing her skin, his silver eyes intent on her body. She shivered convulsively, resenting the power of her own desires, wondering with fierce bitterness why they had chosen now to manifest themselves so strongly. If she had to suffer this kind of delayed adolescent development, why on earth did she have to pick on Silas Jeffreys? Why couldn't she have felt like this about someone safe like . . . like Malcolm? She dwelled bitterly on the recalcitrance of her own nature and its stubborn refusal to behave sensibly. A discreet, easily controlled affair with someone like Malcolm, now at this stage in her life when she was well-established on the career ladder, would have been almost ideal. A relationship which could be picked up and then dropped to suit them both . . . a comfortable physical communion between two people who were fully aware that their relationship was to be kept safely compartmentalised . . . a healthy, unemotional, physical pleasuring of one another. She dwelt bitterly on the benefits of such a relationship while she prepared for bed, wondering a little savagely why on earth she couldn't act on her own sane, sensible advice. Why on earth was she suffering from this inconvenient attack of desire? To merely experience such desire was bad enough, but to have that desire fixated on the one person it would be career suicide to become involved with must be some form of hitherto unsuspected madness.

It was just fortunate that Silas had no interest in her as a woman. She shuddered to think of the consequences to her carefully planned life had that not been the case. An affair with him, no matter how brief, would mean the end of her career with the Jeffreys Group. She had always been appalled by the stupidity of those of her peers who became emotionally or sexually involved with co-workers. It always led to problems—accusations of favouritism and worse. And then, when the inevitable end of the affair came . . . Well, she had listened to too many women bemoaning the fact that they were almost being forced to look for another job following the end of their relationship with a colleague to have any doubts as to her own situation under similar circumstances.

Yes, she was very fortunate indeed that Silas wasn't interested in her. Extremely fortunate. Determinedly she ignored the small pang of pain and chagrin that whispered dangerously that she *could* make him see her as a woman and not a colleague, that she *should* make him see her as a woman.

Wearily she prepared for bed, praying mentally that tonight her sleep would be free of dreams, tormenting and subtle sensual shadows that moved across her sleep, arousing her with the eroticism of their movements, with the way their sleep-misted bodies moved together, touching, clinging . . .

CHAPTER SIX

WHEN she woke up on Thursday morning, Hannah realised that the weather had changed and that the hitherto mild Indian summer they had been enjoying had been replaced by rough winds and a storm-grey sky. Beyond her living-room window, the wind whipped the Thames into white-capped ruffles. Trees which had seemed green only the day before, as though summer would last for ever, now rattled, dry as paper, and the few people she could see moving about were dressed warmly in autumn clothes.

More from habit than deliberate choice, because she never wore her City clothes when she went home, she dressed almost automatically in a warm pleated skirt in bright blues and greens, lightened by a fine broken yellow line which matched the sweater she was wearing with it. There was also a jacket which she had placed on the back of her chair, ready to put on when she went out.

She ate her breakfast quickly, with one eye on the clock. They were travelling down to Padley in Silas's car, and a little to her surprise he had announced that instead of meeting her at the office he would pick her up at home. When she had protested that this was unnecessary, he had reminded her wryly that by picking her up at home he was saving them both almost an extra hour of travelling, and after that there had been no further possible argument.

Even though she had been watching for him, she still felt a small thrill of shock and pleasure in her stomach when she eventually saw his car draw up outside. Sooner or later she was going to stop reacting like this every time she saw him, she told herself stoically, ignoring the tiny curling sensation of awareness that coiled through her muscles.

She arrived downstairs in the foyer almost at the same time as Silas walked into it. He gave her a brief smile, holding out his hand to take the overnight bag she had packed the previous evening. Shaking her head, she responded to his smile and told him, 'It's all right. It's quite light. I can carry it myself.'

He didn't argue with her, instead opening the door so that she could precede him through it, and then unlocking the boot of his car. This time when he held out his hand, she let him take her bag. He stowed it efficiently in the car next to a very similar one of his own, and then walked round to the passenger side, opening the door for her.

'It shouldn't take us long to reach Padley, not once we're clear of the London traffic,' he informed her, reversing the Daimler and heading back to the main road. 'While we're travelling, I'll tell you a bit about my plans for the house. At the moment it's more or less gutted. The builders are hoping to move in at the beginning of next month, and once they're there, they reckon it's going to take them at least six months to get everything in order.'

Hannah frowned. 'Won't you find it very difficult living there with the builders in?' she queried.

'Living there?' He gave her a rather startled glance, and then looked away as he negotiated a very sharp corner. 'I don't *live* there. The place is enormous, far too large for one person. I live in the Dower House.'

Hannah remembered what her mother had said about Padley Court being almost uninhabitable, and gave him a querying look.

'What do you intend to do with it, then?' she asked him, visions of a hotel complex or conference facilities of some sort being developed in the beautiful old house and grounds, and unwillingly acknowledging that, despite the good business sense of such a move, she would be sad to see the gracious old place turned into yet another prestige hotel.

'I intend to turn it into a holiday home for single-parent families,' Silas told her, astounding her.

Her mouth dropped and she turned to stare at him. Although he was concentrating on the traffic, there was nothing in his profile to indicate that he was teasing her.

'You don't approve?' he queried, obviously mistaking her shock for disapproval. 'You're not the only one. I've had to do some pretty heavy fighting with the local council to get them to agree to my proposal. Some of them seem to think the words "one-parent family" are synonymous with delinquent children and uncaring mothers,' he added very bitterly. 'However, I managed to get the plans passed. Luckily I had the support of a very powerful local landowner. I personally won't be running the place, of course. I've appointed, or will appoint, a board of trustees to do that. I will be one of the trustees, but needless to say I won't be able to give the venture my full-time attention. I've bought the parkland with the house and several acres of land, not enough to farm on a profitable basis, but certainly enough to keep a few animals, the idea being that city children would be given a taste of traditional country life through various charitable organisations all over the country.

'We hope to be able to offer to those who are most in need of it one week and in some cases two weeks' holiday at no expense to themselves. I'm sorry if the idea doesn't meet with your approval,' he added a trifle drily when she said nothing.

Not meet with her approval? Hannah could only stare at him belligerently, wondering how on earth she had managed to convey to him such an impression that he considered her so devoid of feeling that she couldn't see how wonderful his idea was.

'Of course I approve,' she told him fiercely. 'I think it's a wonderful idea.'

'Good.' He glanced at her, giving her a genuinely warm smile. 'I'm glad about that, because I'm hoping to more or less put you in charge of the day-to-day organisation and control of the building work. I'll be giving you an assistant to help you with all the paperwork that will be involved, but unless it's something that needs my direct attention, everyone concerned in the work on the place will report directly to you.'

That he should have enough faith in her to give

her such responsibility almost took Hannah's breath away. It was a project dearer to her heart than anything she had ever worked on before. She could feel the adrenalin pumping excitedly through her veins at the thought of the challenges ahead of her, and then she checked and said uncertainly, 'But you employed me as your personal assistant——'

'Which you will still be,' Silas assured her calmly. 'That is why I'm giving you an assistant to help you with the day-to-day paperwork involved in the scheme.'

They were deeply enmeshed in the business of the London traffic and Hannah sat back in her seat, her mind buzzing with ideas and questions, none of which she wanted to put to Silas while he was concentrating so intently on his driving.

She couldn't wait to reach Padley and see for herself just exactly what he intended to do. She knew the estate only very vaguely, having visited it as a child with her parents when they had gone round the gardens. A thought suddenly struck her, and she asked quickly, 'The gardens. What will happen to those? They're on show to the public normally, several times a year.'

'They only occupy a very small part of the estate,' Silas told her calmly. 'They will be out of bounds to the children and maintained as they are now by a small workforce. They will still be open to the public; in fact, we're hoping to open them on a far more regular basis. We're also considering establishing several workshops in some of the outbuildings to the house, hopefully encouraging local craftsmen to set up business there and perhaps even employ some of the older teenagers of the families who will be making use of the place's facilities. The leisure market is booming at the moment, and of course, the more funds we attract to the place, the easier the job of the trustees will be.'

'How will it be financed?' Hannah asked him curiously.

'Largely by private donations.' His voice was clipped, warning her that he didn't want her to pursue her line of questioning, and Hannah suspected instinctively that the major proportion of those private subscriptions would come from Silas himself.

She wondered how much his own childhood with his aunt had influenced his decision to make such an altruistic gesture.

'Tonight we'll be having dinner with the landowner I was telling you about, and his wife. There are several points concerning the eventual running of the place that I want to go over with him. You may know him already: Lord Charles Redvers.'

Hannah shook her head. 'I've heard of him, of course, Redvers Hall is only about thirty miles from my parents' village, but I don't think I've ever actually met him.'

She had also heard about Lord Redvers' wife, Fiona, a very beautiful woman, some twenty years her husband's junior, who it was rumoured had had several discreet affairs during the course of her marriage to Lord Redvers. Hannah didn't place too much credence on this latter information. Small villages were notorious hotbeds of gossip, so she didn't mention Lady Redvers and instead asked Silas how he had come to meet the peer.

'The agents who sold me Padley Court put me in touch with him. I've been on the lookout for a place like Padley for quite some time, and before I bought it I advised the agents exactly what I planned to do with it. They warned me that I would come up against quite a lot of local opposition, but they recommended that I get in touch with Lord Redvers, who I believe has something of a reputation as a philanthropist locally.'

This much was true. Hannah had heard her father mention Lord Redvers as a very generous benefactor of several local charities.

While Hannah remembered Padley Gardens from her visit with her parents as a child, she had no real conception of the house itself, and therefore it came as rather a shock to see how enormous it was. No wonder Silas had been surprised to hear that she believed that he was going to live in it himself.

He turned in through the open drive gates, his car crunching slowly over the gravel. Ahead of them the Tudor brick bulk of the huge house dominated the landscape, its mullioned windows reflecting the sunlight as the sun finally managed to pierce the grey blanket of cloud. The avenue of limes that led to the house was an awe-inspiring sight, despite several gaps in its symmetry, betraying where trees had died over the centuries. But, instead of driving down the avenue, Silas turned off to the left along a bumpy, unmade track.

'Once the builders start work I'm going to have a proper drive made to the Dower House,' he told her, moderating the speed of the car to lessen the effect of the rutted lane.

'How old is the Dower House?' Hannah asked him, not remembering it from previous visits.

'Not as old as the house. It was built early in the eighteenth century, apparently designed by a pupil of Inigo Jones. It isn't overly large: three storeys, with five bedroms on the first floor and then another four on the second. It's also got cellars, which I plan to use to house the computer equipment I'll need to work from home.'

Curiously Hannah asked him, 'When you bought Padley, didn't it occur to you that you could perhaps use it as your head office?'

He shook his head decisively.

'No, it's far too large, for one thing. For another, it wouldn't be fair to the rest of the staff. Central London might be an expensive location to be based in, but it does have certain advantages. If we relocated out here, we would be bound to lose some key members of staff who simply wouldn't be able to travel. Here we are,' he announced, swinging the car round, and Hannah gasped as she had her first glimpse of the Dower House.

Although Silas had described it as relatively small, it was in fact a very substantial building, designed, as he had already informed her, after the school of Inigo Jones, with perfectly proportioned windows and a graciously austere exterior with shallow steps leading up to the impressive porticoed entrance.

'I haven't had much time to do anything about

the inside yet,' he warned her as he stopped the car on the gravel forecourt in front of the house. 'It's habitable rather than comfortable. On the days when I'm working from here, a Mrs Parkinson comes in from the village to give the place a clean-through and to prepare any meals that might be required.'

He released himself from his seat-belt and got out of the car with one easy, graceful movement which Hannah envied as she continued to struggle a little with hers. She had her hand on the handle of the car door when he appeared outside and opened it for her. Thoroughly flustered, she allowed him to help her from the car, cross with herself for the way she was reacting to his proximity. It wasn't even as though she was unused to such small, good-mannered formalities, so why all the nervous reaction and desperate attempt to avoid any contact with him as he reached into the car and placed his hand under her elbow, making it easier for her to step outside?

Why? Did she really need to ask herself that question? she derided herself mentally. She already knew quite well why—why it was that when Silas touched her a rash of fiery darts tingled through her skin and her heart started beating at almost twice its normal rate. Why her stomach churned and her heart seemed to leap and turn over beneath her ribs. Why her whole body seemed to come alive and why danger signals flashed despairingly from her brain.

'Are you all right?' he asked her solicitously. 'You look a little bit pale.'

'A headache,' Hannah fibbed, guiltily, already

aware he was standing far too close to her, scrutinising her far too intently, and that if she didn't pull away from him very soon she was all too likely to betray exactly what it was that was wrong with her. Despairingly she pulled away from him, watching a small frown crease his forehead and the coolness lighten the silver of his eyes.

He had every right to feel annoyed with her. She was behaving like an adolescent, although she suspected he was probably putting her behaviour down to some feminist impulses that would not allow her to accept even the smallest courtesy from him. He was so wrong, but she couldn't tell him that.

'After lunch, I'll show you round the grounds,' he told her curtly. 'A little bit of fresh air should help with your headache, unless of course you'd rather go straight up to your room and lie down for half an hour.'

Hannah shook her head, appalled by his response to her deceit.

'It's nothing,' she assured him, this time truthfully. 'I'm sure it will go almost straight away.'

The front door was already opening as they approached it, a small, plump woman standing in the shadows of the hall. As Hannah stepped inside she caught her breath in pleasure, looking upwards, following the line of the gracefully curved, wrought-iron balustrade. Her heels rang noisily on the traditionally lozenge-tiled black and white floor.

The hall had at some stage been panelled, and the panels were now painted in a flat cream emulsion that did nothing for them. She must have wrinkled her nose in distaste almost without being aware of it, because suddenly at her side Silas said grimly, 'I quite agree. Atrocious, isn't it? One of the first things I intend to do as soon as I can get round to it is to have these panels stripped back to their natural wood finish. Good morning, Mrs Parkinson,' he greeted the other woman, introducing Hannah to her and then suggesting to Mrs Parkinson that she took Hannah upstairs and showed her which bedroom she had been allocated.

'It's just a buffet lunch, Mr Jeffreys,' Mrs Parkinson told him as she smiled at Hannah and walked towards the staircase. 'You did say something light, because you were dining out this evening.'

'That will be fine, Mrs Parkinson,' Silas assured her. 'I want to show Hannah round the grounds and the house itself later on this afternoon. While Mrs Parkinson shows you to your room, I'm going to go to check the answering machine,' he announced to Hannah. 'Take your time. There's no need to rush back downstairs.'

'It's this way, Miss Maitland,' Mrs Parkinson said formally to Hannah, preceding her up the stairs.

She was cheerful and friendly, and obviously thoroughly enjoyed working for Silas. It seemed she knew all about his plans for the big house, and although she was quite frank about the opposit-ion of some of the more hardliners among the villagers it seemed to Hannah that on balance most of the locals approved of what Silas intended to do.

'It stands to reason that the ordinary folk will

be pleased,' Mrs Parkinson announced a little breathlessly as they reached the first-floor landing and she waited for Hannah to join her. 'Something like that means work, and that's something we're short of around here.'

'I know,' Hannah agreed. 'My family live just over fifty miles away.' She went on to explain just who her father was, and Mrs Parkinson said that she seemed to have heard of the vicar.

'I've got a cousin who lives over that way,' she went on to tell Hannah. 'A regular churchgoer she is, too. It's this room, miss.' She stopped outside one of the doors and opened it for Hannah.

The room was enormous, all faded elegance and so evocative of a bygone age that Hannah felt that she could almost smell the dry old scent of lavender in the air. As well as the elegant French empire four-poster, the room also boasted a day-bed elegantly covered in silk damask, now faded and worn in places, but still possessed of the richness that made it impossible for Hannah to resist touching it with her fingers. The bed was draped in the same fabric with a matching coverlet, both of them probably priceless.

Hannah suspected that they must be part of the original fittings of the house, and this was confirmed when Mrs Parkinson informed her that Silas had bought the house with all of its contents.

'I'll leave you up here to unpack,' she told Hannah. 'Mr Jeffreys normally likes lunch at twelve-thirty prompt.'

'I shan't be as long as that,' Hannah assured her.

'It will only take me a few minutes to unpack my bag. Where do I go when I come downstairs?' she asked the older woman, listening carefully as Mrs Parkinson gave her rather obscure directions.

All she had brought with her was a change of underwear, her jeans and casual clothes to wear over the weekend while she was staying with her parents, and nothing that was at all suitable for wearing for going out to dinner. She frowned a little over this error on her own part, wishing that she had had the forethought to pack a simple dress in her bag.

It was too late now to worry about it. She would simply have to go out to dinner in what she was wearing. However, she reflected that to Silas her lack of attention to such a detail might hint that she was not quite as efficient as she ought to be. She was still frowning over this when she went downstairs, hesitating as she reached the bottom step, not quite sure from Mrs Parkinson's directions exactly where she was supposed to go.

Her dilemma was solved for her when one of the doors off the hall suddenly opened and Silas came out.

'Ah, good. I thought those were your footsteps I heard on the stairs,' he announced, smiling at her.

Like her, he was dressed in comfortable rather than city clothes, trousers in a mixture of wool and what she suspected was very probably silk in a faintly tweedy design. It went well with the oatmeal sweater he was wearing over his sports shirt. She had noticed a leather jacket thrown casually on the back seat of the car.

'I'm using this room as my study,' he informed her, holding the door open and gesturing to her to go in. Obediently she did so.

The room looked out over the side of the house, with views across the parkland to the main house in the distance. In style it was very similar to his office in London, although here the fabrics were very faded and the furnishings rather more battered. The Aubusson rug on the floor had holes in it and thread-bare patches, but none of that detracted in the slightest from the delightful warmth of the room. There was even a fire burning in the grate, and he smiled when he saw her looking at it.

'As yet, the house doesn't have the benefits of any form of central heating, so Mrs Parkinson knows to light fires whenever I come down. It helps to keep the house aired, apart from anything else. Oh, and before we get involved in anything else, one or two points about tonight. We'll be dining with Lord Redvers in his own home. Although he hasn't said, I suspect we probably won't be the only dinner guests. I'm hoping to have the opportunity to have a few words with him in private before we leave.

'Naturally I'll introduce you to him as my assistant, but he's one of the old school and you might find yourself relegated to the drawing-room and the teacups.' He saw that she was frowning and smiled ruefully at her.

'Do you disapprove? I'm not surprised. I suspect you think I should take issue with Lord Redvers and inform him that today's woman quite rightfully expects due appreciation to be made of the fact that she is every bit as intelligent as her male counterpart. However, in this instance, I feel it would be unwise to antagonise him. It's really only his support that's swinging the county die-hards over to our point of view.'

Hannah checked him quickly. 'It isn't that.'

As soon as Silas had mentioned that they might not be the only people dining with Lord and Lady Redvers, her concern regarding suitable lack of clothing had increased. Normally it wouldn't have mattered, but she was very much aware that she was a representative of the company, and that as such she ought to be dressed accordingly.

'What is it, then?' Silas asked her.

She gave him an apologetic look. 'I'm sorry, but it just never occurred to me that we might be dining out formally, and I haven't brought with me anything suitable to wear.'

'Ah.' For a moment she almost thought he was actually going to laugh at her, but if he was indeed amused he managed to conceal it from her.

'Of course I'm quite happy to wear the outfit I have on now——' she told him stiffly.

'No, you can't do that.' He cut right across what she had been going to say with a decisive shake of his head. 'Lord Redvers is a stickler for form. It's my fault, really. I should have warned you to bring an outfit suitable for evening wear with you. In fact, I did intend to mention it to Maggie—but the problem isn't insoluble,' he told her firmly, after a second consideration. 'We're only about ten miles from Shaftesbury. You can take the car and drive over there this afternoon and buy something suitable to wear.'

Hannah looked as shocked as she felt.

'Drive your car?' she protested. 'Oh, no, I couldn't do that.'

He gave her an extremely dry look.

'Why not? There might, after all, be occasions when you have to. If you haven't got a credit card with you, I'll give you a cheque.'

Quickly Hannah shook her head. 'No. It's all right, I've . . .'

'The company will pay for the outfit, Hannah,' he interrupted her firmly. 'Let's not waste any time arguing about this.' He glanced at his watch. 'We've got one hell of a lot to get through this afternoon. I suggest you go to Shaftesbury. I've got some papers here in my briefcase that I can be going through while you've gone. I think I can spare you for about an hour, an hour and a half at the most.'

Once again Hannah discovered she was being put in a position where it was impossible to argue with him. The buffet lunch Mrs Parkinson had mentioned to them was set out in what Silas described as the original breakfast-room to the house—a pretty, pleasantly sized room overlooking the rear courtyard, and which he explained to her caught the early-morning sun.

The buffet was substantial enough to feed a workforce far in excess of theirs. Hannah picked nervously at the contents of her own plate, wondering if Silas was regretting bringing her with him. So far during the short period of her employment with him she seemed to have made her fair share of mistakes. It was impossible to read anything from his shuttered expression, but as soon as she possibly could she drank the last of her coffee and got up, saying unsteadily, 'I'll go to Shaftesbury now, then, shall I?'

His eyebrows lifted. 'If you're sure you've had enough to eat. I'm not a slave-driver, Hannah,' he pointed out drily.

'I'm not hungry,' she assured him truthfully. 'I never eat a large meal during the day.'

He reached into his trouser pocket to remove his car keys, the movement drawing the pocket tautly against the muscles of his thighs. As she followed the small movement, Hannah felt her face start to burn with conscious awareness of both him and her reaction to him.

She looked away hurriedly, furious with herself for her idiotic and unprofessional behaviour.

'I'll be back just as soon as I can,' she assured him, taking the keys from him. They were still warm from their intimate contact with his body, and as she closed her hand around them she felt her palm start to sweat slightly in nervous awareness.

Luckily she already knew the way to Shaftesbury, and the Daimler, once she had got used to its small idiosyncrasies, proved a joy to drive. She parked in a large car park just outside the main shopping centre, checking carefully to make sure the car was securely locked before hurrying towards the shops.

It would be just her luck to find that none of the shops had anything remotely suitable, she reflected crossly as she glanced in the window of the first one she came to, and dismissed the outfits she saw there. A quarter of an hour later she had almost reached the point of total despair. So far every shop she had seen had been totally unable to provide her with what she needed, and then, just as she was about to give up, she rounded a corner into a narrow alleyway and discovered tucked away there a small shopfront that boasted one simple outfit, a plain black dress with a tulip-shaped skirt, long sleeves and a slightly scooped neckline.

She knew the moment she saw it that it would be absolutely ideal, and she found as she walked into the shop that she was holding her breath, hardly daring to hope that they might have it in her size.

The girl inside the shop listened sympathetically as she explained her plight. The dress was part of their new autumn stock, she told Hannah, and she would have to check on the size. After she had done so, she gave Hannah a warm smile.

'You're in luck,' she told her. 'We've only got two of this particular style. One of them I happen to know is a fourteen. This one is the ten.'

Hannah let out her breath in a shaky sigh of relief, waiting while the girl deftly removed the dress from the model. She tried it on quickly in the privacy of one of the two cubicles, relieved to discover that it fitted her perfectly.

When she came out to study her reflection in the long mirror, the salesgirl's eyes opened wide in admiration.

'It looks stunning,' she assured Hannah truthfully.

It was expensive enough to make Hannah grimace

a little as she paid for it. Despite what Silas had said, she had no intention of allowing the company to reimburse her for the cost. A brief sortie back in the main shopping area provided her with a pair of high-heeled black suede court shoes and some sheer black tights.

'Manage to get anything?' Silas asked her as she hurried breathlessly from the car into his study. The desk was littered with papers, and it occurred to Hannah that he looked almost tired, something she had never noticed before. He always seemed to exude energy, and she had somehow or other come to believe that he was almost superhuman in his physical and mental resources.

Now as she looked at him she could see the frown lines of concentration on his forehead, and the weariness lying in shadows in the depths of his eyes.

'Well, you've certainly made good time,' he told her, standing up, stretching, lively as a panther, his muscles cracking as he lifted his arms above his head. 'If you're ready, I'll take you over to the main house and show you around.'

He tapped a cylindrical roll of papers on his desk. 'These are the plans. We'll take them with us so that you can see what we're planning to do.'

He stepped back to allow her to precede him through the door, but Hannah hesitated, accidentally bumping into him. She froze instinctively as her body came into contact with his, every muscle tense against the all too familiar sensation the contact brought. She saw him frown as she stepped back from him, muttering an apology, and was conscious that she had displeased him with her clumsiness.

'Perhaps I'd better lead the way,' he said tersely, stepping past her into the hall.

Numbly Hannah followed him, miserably aware of his almost instant recoil from contact with her.

CHAPTER SEVEN

AS SHE followed him down the gravel drive, Hannah was glad she had changed her high heels for more comfortable flat shoes. Close to, she could see the dilapidation that time had wrought on the soft brick façade of the house. Darker patches of colour on the walls showed where ivy had once grown. The soft sandstone mullions were worn away in places, and Silas explained to her that these were going to be repaired.

Part of the trustees' work would be to get as many suppliers as possible to supply them free of charge.

As they walked into the house, a thin beam of sunlight which had pierced the grey clouds and highlighted the rich colour of the brickwork disappeared. Already the first of the season's leaves were beginning to drift down on to the driveway.

Inside, the hall was dark and gloomy, small Tudor windows allowing in only a small amount of daylight. Panelling similar to that at the Dower House clothed the walls of the large rectangular room. It had an ornately plastered ceiling and an enormous fireplace in roughly hewn stone, with a date and the arms of whoever had commissioned it carved into it. The few pieces of heavy, dusty furniture scattered round the room looked forlorn.

'I know, it doesn't look very welcoming at the

moment, does it?' Silas commented, grimacing a little. 'We'll go into the drawing-room and I'll show you the plans.'

Hannah followed him, avoiding the small heaps of rubble on the floor, through a series of ornately carved doors into a room which had windows overlooking both the front and the side of the house. The room was furnished with several settees and some chairs, all of them covered with large sheets of calico. Silas headed for a battered oak table, unrolling the plans as he reached it.

'This is what we're hoping to do,' he told Hannah, speaking to her over his shoulder. 'Come and have a look.'

She approached him cautiously, not wanting to get too close to him, and when she stood hesitantly several feet away from him he frowned and said curtly, 'You can't see anything from there. Come here, closer.'

He didn't seem to be satisfied until they were standing practically shoulder to shoulder, Hannah so tensely aware of the heat emanating from his flesh to her own that, even though she was staring down at the plans, none of the lines drawn on them made the slightest sense to her. She tried to concentrate on what Silas was saying about splitting up the large bedrooms into smaller, more compact units, and thought she was doing quite well, until he suddenly said in exasperation, 'You're not looking at the right place. It's here that I'm talking about.' His forefinger jabbed impatiently at one of the drawings, and before she could guess what he intended to do his other hand reached out and cupped her face, turning it ungently in the direction in which he was pointing.

The shock of the unexpected and unwanted physical contact obliterated everything else. She could almost literally feel her bones turn soft and liquid, and her body tremble under the onslaught of the sensations even his most casual physical contact with her caused. She started to tremble, totally unable to stop the physical reaction of her body. His hand tensed a little against her face, and he subjected her to a hard-eyed scrutiny before saying curtly, 'You're cold. We'll cut this as short as we can, and then I'll show you round the place. That might give you a better idea of what we're undertaking.'

This time, when he turned his attention to the plans, Hannah forced herself to concentrate on what he was saying and to ignore her body's awareness of the hard jut of his hips against her softer flesh. The powerful structure of his body, as he shifted his weight from one foot to the other, brushed even more closely against her. She almost shook with relief when he finally started to roll up the plans.

'We'll start at the top and work our way down,' he told her, his voice still curt, and she had the unhappy conviction that her inability to concentrate on the plans was probably making him wonder if he had after all made the right decision in employing her.

'Be careful on the stairs,' he warned her as he waited for her at the base of them. 'Some of them are starting to rot away. The builders have put crosses on the most dangerous ones, but I'll go up first just to be on the safe side.'

The staircase itself was richly carved with swags of fruit and garlands so real that Hannah stopped on one of the stairs in awe to reach out and trace the petals of a dusty flower, wondering at the artistry and dedication of the long-ago workman who had originally conceived and executed the design. Above her, Silas stopped as well, looking down at her absorbed face with an expression that was both illuminating and guarded.

'Grinling Gibbons?' Hannah hazarded, making a guess at the identity of that long-ago workman.

Silas shook his head, 'Good guess, but no, it wasn't actually Grinling Gibbons himself, but one of his pupils.' He gave her a wry grimace. 'The work came cheaper that way, apparently. We've been lucky enough to find in one of the old chests a whole host of household accounts, one of them relating to the cost of this particular staircase. Fortunately, most of it is still intact. It's the stairs themselves that have suffered the most deterioration. Watch out,' he added warningly as Hannah, still admiring the carving, didn't look where she was going and put her foot on one of the chalk-marked stairs.

Immediately she checked, freezing where she was, and instinctively Silas reached out to take hold of her arm and steady her. As she swayed slightly, reacting to the strong pressure of his fingers curling round her wrist, he came down to her level, supporting her with one arm round her shoulders, his forehead furrowed in a frown as he asked swiftly, 'Are you all right?'

'I'm fine,' Hannah lied firmly, feeling an absolute fool for having forgotten his warning about the stairs. 'I'm sorry,' she added shakily. 'You must think me an absolute idiot, but I was so engrossed in the carving that I forgot to look out for the cross.'

'Don't worry about it,' he told her. 'If I hadn't called out so sharply, you'd probably have noticed it for yourself. For a moment there, I thought you were going to lose your balance and fall backwards.'

'No danger of that happening,' Hannah assured him, striving to appear normal and relaxed while at the same time very conscious of the weight of his arm around her shoulder and the heavy, even thud of his heart almost against her cheek. So close, in fact, that the temptation to lean against him was almost overpowering. It was straining her mental resources to their absolute limit to try to appear anything like normal. 'I'm not insured for that kind of accident,' she added in what she hoped passed for a joking manner.

'The company is,' Silas assured her tersely, 'but a possible insurance claim was the last thing on my mind.'

At some stage he had discarded his sweater, and his leather jacket was open so that when he had reached out instinctively to take hold of her he had curved her face and body into the protection of his, and now that her first fright at the thought of falling was over, Hannah found that with every breath that she took she was drawing into herself the unique and erotic scent of his body. It was having a dismaying effect on her senses.

Beneath her own sweater she could feel her breasts swell and push eagerly against the confines of her bra. Her nipples felt hard and a little sore, and she was thankful she was wearing her jacket so that her arousal was safely concealed.

She started to pull away from Silas, all too conscious of the fact that she was practically leaning against him, almost revelling in the close proximity of his body, and surely for far longer than was strictly necessary under the circumstances. But to her surprise, instead of immediately releasing her, his fingers seemed to curl and tighten on her shoulder, almost as though he was reluctant to let her go. Unable to stop herself, she allowed herself to savour the pleasure of the moment, unaware of the fact that she was almost nestling against him as she gave a faint sigh and let her body relax completely against his.

Again his arm tightened, this time his fingers almost bruising her softer flesh. She felt his head move and one hand brushed her hair lightly as he leaned towards her ear and asked anxiously, 'Are you sure you're all right? Would you prefer not to go on?'

The effect of his words, spoken so close to the delicate spirals of her ear, made her shudder compulsively. Somehow or other, her hand was resting against the front of his shirt, and beneath the soft fabric she could feel hard bone and muscle. He breathed deeply, as though he too was sharing her sexually induced tension, and then shockingly she realised where she was and what she was doing, and she pulled away from him with a faint gasp, only just remembering to answer his question as she said quickly, 'No, I'm fine. Let's go on.' That was, after all, what she was here for, she reminded herself, as he turned away from her without a word and started to remount the stairs.

The rest of the afternoon passed very quickly indeed, and Hannah soon found herself catching Silas's enthusiasm for his plans for the house. Already a great deal of private money had been raised to help finance the project, and although Silas had contributed to the plans personally by buying the house in the first place, he had also managed to persuade the directors of the Jeffreys Group to vote a certain percentage of each year's profits towards running the completed property.

Her physical desire for him would have been easier to live with if she did not admire him so much as a fellow human being, Hannah acknowledged unhappily as they headed back to the Dower House. Liking him, respecting him, admiring him for all that he was doing, for his charity and philanthropy towards others less fortunate than himself, could only add to her problems.

If she could merely desire him without liking him, it would have been so much easier to isolate those unwanted and treacherous feelings that seemed to have sprung up inside her, like so many deep-rooted weeds, refusing to be torn out and destroyed.

During the course of their tour, Hannah had made copious notes, determined to banish what she felt sure must be Silas's opinion of her inefficiency by proving to him how professional she could be. They got back to the Dower House just as it started to rain.

Mrs Parkinson was just on the point of leaving. Her husband had come to pick her up, and pleasantries were exchanged between the two men as he and Silas chatted for a few minutes while Mrs Parkinson told her that she had left a tray of tea and some sandwiches in the kitchen, just in case they needed anything to eat. She also added that she had set the fire in the study, following a weather bulletin that warned of a sharp drop of temperature overnight.

Silas, who had overheard this last comment, said ruefully to Hannah after Mr and Mrs Parkinson had left, 'I'm afraid you're not getting the best possible introduction to Padley. Luckily we do have a boiler that provides gallons of hot water, but I'm afraid you might find the house itself rather chilly.'

'I doubt it,' Hannah assured him, glad at last to be able to show him a more positive side of her personality. 'I grew up in a house without central heating. In fact, my parents still claim that they actually prefer to do without it except in the very coldest of conditions. It was installed a couple of years ago, and my mother complains that every winter since, both she and my father have had more than their fair share of colds.'

'Well, you won't suffer from cold tonight, at

least,' Silas told her. 'Lord Redvers believes in the American ideal of keeping his home heated to sub-tropical temperatures, possibly because Fiona, his wife, is half-American.'

He glanced at his watch. 'We've got a couple of hours before we need to think about getting ready. Did I hear Mrs P say something about there being a tray of tea in the kitchen?'

'Yes,' Hannah agreed. 'Would you like me to go and get it?'

His manner towards not just her but towards her entire sex was such that she felt no pressure from him to conform to a male and chauvinistic ideal of a woman's responsibility in offering to perform this small chore, but, not completely to her surprise, Silas shook his head.

'No, that's all right. I'll go and do it. Despite what you've said about the lack of central heating, I can see that you're beginning to shiver a little bit. You go and sit down in the study and I'll bring tea.'

Hannah didn't argue with him, and this time when he unrolled the plans for the house she was able to follow his description of the various alterations they were putting in hand, and the work schedule that would have to be followed, with much greater clarity and ease than she had done before. She refused to allow herself to acknowledge that this might have something to do with the fact that they now had the width of the table between them, and that she was safely distant from the all too dangerous proximity of his body and the effect it could have on her.

By seven o'clock it was completely dark outside. There was something undeniably comforting about sitting in front of a well-burning log fire, with the rain pattering audibly on the windows outside, Hannah acknowledged as she stretched luxuriously in her chair, unaware that Silas was watching her until her said in an amused voice, 'When you do that you remind me of a sleek, elegant cat, all feline grace and satisfaction.'

Since to Hannah the picture his words conjured up was so totally at odds with her own image of herself, she immediately froze. For some reason the words he had used had instantly made her think of the soft, almost boneless sensuality she had so often noticed in her mother's domestic cat, and her skin flushed as she stood up a little abruptly, saying hurriedly, 'I think it's time I went upstairs and got changed.'

As she made to walk past him, Silas reached out and held her arm lightly. 'It's all right, Hannah,' he told her rather drily. 'Just because I pass the odd compliment, it doesn't mean that I'm about to pounce on you, you know.'

She immediately flushed a dark, betraying pink, unable to stop a fierce rush of blood up under her skin.

'I didn't think you were,' she told him swiftly, totally unable to look at him.

'No?' His eyebrows rose.

Quite without knowing why Hannah persisted, 'I was just a little surprised by your compliment.'

She struggled for the words to tell him why, without totally betraying what she was thinking, when he astounded her by saying almost curtly, 'Why? Aren't I allowed to be a man as well as a boss, Hannah? Am I supposed to pretend that I'm totally unaware of you as a very desirable woman?'

Hannah could scarcely believe her ears. She stared at him, searching his face for some betraying sign that he was making fun of her, but couldn't find any.

'I . . .' She tried to speak, and discovered that her throat was clogged. She swallowed nervously and tried again, but before she could say anything the phone rang.

'You're right,' Silas told her, walking over to his desk to pick up the receiver. 'It is time to get ready. We don't want to be late, and it's a good three-quarters of an hour's drive.'

He gave her a brisk, almost dismissive nod as he spoke curtly into the receiver and, taking the hint, Hannah opened the door and stepped through it. All the time she was getting ready to go out, she could hardly concentrate on what she was doing. She was totally baffled by Silas's attitude towards her—that he should compliment her, and even more that he should actually imply that he found her attractive; both these things were so out of context with what she had previously seen to be his behaviour towards the female members of his staff.

What did it mean? Was he perhaps just testing her?

Her unease grew as she prepared for dinner. Silas was no monk. She had already heard discreet whispers around the offices concerning the woman who had so far shared his life. Not perhaps by modern standards an excessive number of them. Two or three longstanding affairs seemed to be the general consensus of opinion, all of them ending by the apparent mutual consent of both parties.

The office grapevine seemed to believe that at the moment there was no one special in Silas's life, but Hannah wasn't so sure. There was that woman she had seen him with in her own village, and there had been something distinctly proprietorial about the way she had laid her hand on Silas's arm. But if the office grapevine was correct, if there wasn't anyone special in Silas's life at the moment, if he was genuinely attracted to her, enough, say, to discreetly institute an affair . . . She gave a tiny shudder of fear. If he did approach her in such a way, would she have the strength to reject him? And, if she found that strength, how would he react to such a rejection? So far he had shown himself to be almost a paragon among his sex, but men were notoriously vulnerable where their egos were concerned.

A rejection from her, no matter how tactfully done, was surely bound to influence her career with the Jeffreys Group. But wasn't she looking too far ahead into the future, making assumptions which were all too probably totally incorrect?

All right, so Silas had described her as physically attractive; that didn't mean necessarily that he desired her. She knew she couldn't allow herself to become emotionally involved with him. To do so would be to risk everything she had striven for.

The depth of the emotional bonding and intensity of need she could already feel stirring within herself ran completely counter to the way she had planned her life. To become involved with Silas as his lover would mean the total destruction of her cherished emotional independence. The truth was, she could not trust herself to have an affair with him and not succumb to the very real instincts she had fought so hard to suppress. Instincts which she already knew went with marriage, children, commitment and all those things which she had so often seen destroy the bright futures of so many members of her sex, as they willingly, joyfully even, set aside their own goals in order to satisfy the needs of others.

Many times she had been told by friends that marriage and children had taken the keen edge off their own ambitions; that they were happier now than they had been at any other time in their lives. They had actually laughed at the doubts she had expressed, and those who somehow, impossibly, managed to combine both high-powered careers and marriage and a family, despite their evident exhaustion, had claimed that the fulfilment experienced through their careers was nothing once compared with what they shared now with their partners and children.

Hannah had remained unconvinced, not so much because she doubted the evidence they were giving her, but because she sensed within herself a terrible threat of dependence which would make it all too easy for someone she loved to dominate her life. Not that she loved Silas, of course; what she felt for him was simply physical desire, a long-delayed experience of adolescence, an inconvenient focusing of all that was feminine within her on his maleness.

He was waiting for her when she went downstairs, and, although traditionally it was supposed to be the man who stood back and gasped at the sight of the woman transformed out of her everyday uniform into a creature of mystery and desire, it was she who hesitated on the stairs, her eyes widening in instinctive acknowledgement of how very good he looked in the impeccable elegance of his dinner-suit and immaculately starched white shirt.

As she dragged her gaze away from him, she acknowledged her desire to simply stand and drink in the sight of him.

Her heart was beating far too fast. She avoided looking directly at him, afraid of what he might read in her eyes.

His calm, 'Ready?' was cool and free of any inflexion at all She told herself she ought to feel relieved that any compliment from him would surely only have reinforced her own doubts and apprehensions, but instead what she did feel was an unmistakable sense of disappointment, of being let down.

'Are you all right?' Silas asked her curtly when she didn't move, his voice striking a cold chill through her body, making her shiver involuntarily.

'Yes,' she responded crisply, and as she followed him out to the car, and waited for him to unlock its doors she asked wryly, 'Is there anything specific

I ought to know about this evening, apart from the fact that Lord Redvers doesn't believe women have a place in the business world?'

'Nothing that I can think of. Ostensibly this evening is simply an invitation to dinner and an opportunity to discuss certain matters appertaining to the redevelopment of Padley. As I've already mentioned, such discussions are likely to take place after dinner.'

'When I will be relegated to the drawing-room and the company of Lady Redvers,' Hannah said challengingly. Just how challengingly she only realised when Silas stopped what he was doing and looked sharply at her.

'I'm sorry if that offends you,' he said silkily, 'but I'm afraid I can't change Lord Redvers' view of the world and women's place in it—nor do I believe I should be held responsible for it,' he added in a deceptively mild tone that told Hannah he had all too clearly read the rebellion of her thoughts.

He had finished unlocking the car, and before he could come round and open her door for her Hannah pulled it open herself, wincing a little as she felt its unexpected weight. It was on the tip of her tongue to suggest that it might be as well if she stayed behind, and that her usefulness this evening as his personal assistant was likely to be non-existent, but because she knew her real reasons for wanting to wriggle out of the evening ahead had nothing to do with her apparent chagrin over Lord Redvers' attitude towards her sex she kept grimly silent.

Her reactions to Silas both angered and confused her. No matter how much she tried to analyse them, to step aside from them and put them in their proper perspective, the moment she saw him all her defences came tumbling down.

She leaned back in her seat, her head on the head-rest, closing her eyes, and then wished immediately that she hadn't, because Silas's face formed in minute detail behind her shuttered eyelids and she had a compulsive suicidal urge to turn to him and touch him. Luckily, she managed to control it.

She opened her eyes and tried to concentrate on more businesslike matters, wishing the evening was already at an end and she was safe in the solitude of her bed, where her renegade emotions were not likely to betray her.

CHAPTER EIGHT

LORD AND LADY REDVERS lived in a rambling, uncoordinated house which had been in his family since the time of the Reformation, and which had been built on the site of a convent which Henry the Eighth had caused to be razed to the ground.

Local rumour had it that the intense ferocity with which Lord Redvers' ancestor had set about the destruction of the original building had more to do with the fact that an heiress he had been desperate to marry had escaped him by entering the convent than with any real zeal for Henry's new religion. Whatever the case, he had certainly profited from that zeal; Henry had granted him the lands on which the convent had originally stood, and the oldest part of the house was said to be built from stones actually taken from the sacked building.

During Charles the Second's time a disciple of Inigo Jones had added a new façade, behind which the original Tudor rooms remained cramped and low-ceilinged. He had also added half a dozen new reception rooms with expensive panelling and even more expensive plasterwork ceilings, and that grandeur had contented the family until the Prince Regent's time, when the then incumbent of the title had married a woman who had decided that the place could only be improved by incorporating some of the Prince Regent's more *outré* ideas; so it was that several of the rooms were decorated in the Regency fad for *chinoiserie* with expensive silks and delicately carved and gilded furniture.

A Victorian Lord Redvers had added an extra wing, and the result was the jumbled sprawl of buildings lining the skyline as Silas turned into the drive past the now unoccupied lodge houses.

Hannah shifted tensely in her seat. She wasn't looking forward to the evening ahead. Silas parked his car next to a very large BMW and commented unemotionally, 'Looks as if we shan't be the only dinner guests.'

It was a statement and didn't invite any comment. Hannah ducked her head as he assisted her out of the car, wishing that she didn't have to touch him, but he had already extended his hand to her and to refuse to take it would have initiated exactly the kind of speculation she had no wish for him to embark on. Even so, she shivered a little at the brief physical contact, causing his mouth to harden abruptly and his fingers to tighten around her so that when she tried to release herself she found that she could not.

From feeling cold she went hot; a kind of heat that began in the pit of her stomach and spread to every part of her body, a melting, yielding heat that made her legs tremble and her heart turn over slowly within her body.

How long they would have stayed there like that in the soft darkness of the autumn evening if the door hadn't opened, trapping them both in a beam of harsh light, she had no idea.

As it was, the shock of that intrusive light, of someone else's unwanted presence, made her panic and pull away, half surprised to find that Silas had already released her. She was facing the house, and as Silas stood to one side she could see into the brilliantly illuminated hallway.

A butler stood imposingly, waiting for them, formidably correct and very aloof. Hannah blinked a little. Given the much publicised new poverty of so many members of the peerage, she had not expected such evidence of wealth.

Someone had transformed—if indeed that was the correct word to describe the desecration of the elegant austerity of the Carolinian hall with its panelled walls, cream stuccoed ceiling and lozenge-tiled floor, hanging the stone-mullioned windows with acres of pastel chintz and befrilled curtains, so out of keeping with the heavy majesty of the house that they made Hannah wince.

As he gave their names to the butler, Silas became aware of her expression and bent his head to whisper warningly, 'Lord Redvers apparently gave his wife *carte blanche* with the décor.' He didn't need to say any more, but Hannah couldn't help giving him a startled glance of distaste for the inappropriateness of the delicate, over-pretty chintz in a room that cried out for worn, heavy damask, for rich scarlets and faded golds.

They were left standing in the large hall while the butler disappeared between a massive set of double doors, presumably to announce their arrival.

It was warm in the hall, too warm, Hannah

reflected, looking a little sadly at the huge empty fireplace and then at the none too discreetly placed radiators that were heating the room to an almost stifling temperature.

A staircase similar to the one in Padley Court, and carved with all manner of mystical creatures and emblems, rose upwards to a galleried landing. While Hannah was studying the carving, the double doors opened again and a small, portly man hurried towards them, greeting Silas warmly.

'Can't think what Pearson was about, leaving you out here,' he apologised brusquely, ushering them through the doors as Silas paused to introduce Hannah to him.

'Hannah Maitland, my assistant, Lord Redvers.'

The peer shook Hannah's hand and peered a little myopically at her. He had kind eyes, Hannah thought, and a rather quizzical-cum-sad, almost canine cast of feature.

'Can't think why we need a butler, anyway, but Fiona seemed to think it necessary. Know my wife at all, do you?' he asked Hannah abruptly.

She shook her head, deeming it unpolitic to tell him that, although she didn't know Lady Redvers personally, she had heard all the local gossip about her.

'Half-American, you know,' he announced, and then shook his head.

Lord Redvers ushered them into a large drawing-room, which Hannah realised instantly must be one of the rooms designed and decorated by his wife. Here again the pretty-pretty chintzes did not do justice to the room, but they were a perfect foil to the woman standing up to greet them. Or rather, not them, but Silas, Hannah recognised bleakly, noting the way Fiona Redvers' eyes flicked over her and then dismissed her.

'Silas, darling! At last. I was beginning to wonder what had happened to you.'

To Hannah she said nothing at all. Not a woman's woman, Hannah acknowledged wryly.

From her position slightly behind Silas, Hannah studied the other woman. She was a little older than Hannah, somewhere in her mid-thirties, Hannah guessed although she adopted the girlish, trilling voice of a much younger woman, and her skilfully applied make-up did much to heighten the onlooker's impression that she was still only in her mid-twenties. This, combined with the cooing voice and fragile, dainty mannerisms, conjured up a vision of delicate, blonde loveliness and fragility which Hannah was pretty sure was totally at variance with the woman's true nature. She was as brittle as overspun glass, and twice as cold, Hannah suspected.

There was a certain obvious hardness in those round, baby-blue eyes, a certain dispassionate and dismissing assessment in the way she studied Hannah from top to toe and then, ignoring her, turned her attention to Silas.

No, she didn't like her, Hannah reflected inwardly. She wasn't the kind of woman she could ever warm to. She wasn't the type of woman who considered her own sex important enough to be worthy of cultivating. And as for female *friends* . . . this was a woman to whom every other member of her sex could only be seen as a foil or an enemy.

'Silas, come and meet some friends of ours,' she invited, tucking her arm cleverly through Silas's and deliberately drawing him away from Hannah, leaving her standing in the middle of the over-decorated, sugary-sweet room, having neglected to introduce her to anyone else, and having effectively seen to it that Hannah was totally isolated from everyone else, since Lord Redvers had gone in search of a drink for them both, and the only other two guests were seated on an overstuffed, pretty, pastel-pink rose-strewn sofa, which Hannah decided nastily they had been deliberately invited to occupy as the roses contrasted disastrously with the female half of the couple's pale gingery hair.

Fiona, in contrast, looked all blonde delicateness against the backdrop of rose-patterned chintz. The white dress she was wearing was surely far too dressy for a simple sixsome dinner party and showed off a tan that was far too even to have been acquired on any beach.

Hannah's chin tilted firmly in defiance as she saw the nervous, pitying glance the ginger-haired woman gave her, almost as though she was used to the bad manners their hostess displayed to the female section of her guests, and, deliberately turning her back on all of them, Hannah walked slowly across to where a group of paintings were displayed on the wall.

Vaguely reminiscent of Canaletto's style, they had a pleasing amateurishness about them that, combined with the dates on them, made Hannah wonder if they had perhaps been painted by some member of Lord Redvers' family, after the fashion of the time.

She was musing on this when Lord Redvers coughed apologetically behind her. She swung round, flushing a little. She had been too engrossed in the paintings to be aware of his presence. He handed her her drink, and said in the abrupt style she was becoming accustomed to, 'Painted by a spinster aunt of the family. Quite good, I thought. Found 'em in the attic and had 'em reframed. Fiona doesn't care for them.'

'I think they're lovely,' Hannah assured him warmly. As she turned towards him, she saw that Silas was standing chatting to the male occupant of the sofa who had now stood up, leaving his wife, if indeed that was their relationship, sitting forlornly on her own, while Fiona stood between the two men, leaning provocatively against Silas, her trilling laughter ringing out every now and again.

Hannah wondered cynically if she and Silas were having an affair. She had recognised her immediately as being the woman she had seen in Silas's car and, whatever Silas's feelings toward her, there was little doubt about hers towards him. Beneath all the sugary sweetness, she was watching him with all the eager sexual hunger of a female praying mantis.

Was it because she herself loved him that she found it so easy to recognise her own need in others? She went rigid abruptly, totally unaware of what Lord Redvers was saying to her. She didn't love him. How could she? Love was something that grew slowly. It needed nourishing, cherishing; it wasn't something that materialised out of nowhere like ectoplasm.

But it had done. She loved him. She loved Silas . . .

The words rang hollowly through her like a death knell. She actually shivered, despite the almost tropical heat of the room, not wanting to admit the truth, not wanting to acknowledge what had happened.

She looked across at Silas wildly, as though desperate to find a denial of her feelings, to look at him and discover that he was after all just another man, but by some unlucky chance, as she looked at him, he looked back at her, and desire, need . . . love itself arced through her like lightning, unmistakable and unchangeable.

Fiona was still talking to him, and he lifted his hand as though commanding her silence. For one heart-stopping moment Hannah actually thought he intended to cross the room and come to her, but then Fiona reached out and touched him as she had done that day in the car, slender, beautifully manicured nails against his sleeves . . . nails that to Hannah were more like claws.

She closed her eyes and shivered, and in the distance heard Fiona's tinkling, unmelodious voice announcing dinner.

The other couple turned out to be one of Lord Redvers' business associates—an architect, whom he wanted Silas to meet, and his wife.

The husband paid more attention to Fiona than his wife, flattering her with such fulsome compliments that Hannah knew if she had been on the receiving end of them she would have instantly put him down. Couldn't he see what he was doing to his wife?

All through dinner Hannah felt her anger grow: against Fiona for being so vainly selfish that she cared not one whit about the misery of the little mousy, ginger-haired wife; the husband, George Mercer, for his lack of consideration for his wife, and for his total and obvious belief that women were the lesser species and that they came in two varieties—those one married and kept domestically at home, and those like Fiona, whom one flirted with and lusted after. She was also angry with Lord Redvers because he seemed not to notice his wife's bad manners. But most of all she was angry with Silas.

Silas, who every now and again detached himself from Fiona's predatory attentions and looked across the table at her, not as George Mercer looked at his wife, but questioningly, affectionately, thoughtfully.

How ironic that she should be forced to acknowledge that she loved him tonight of all nights, when she was forced to witness everything she detested about woman's portion of the marital state.

She looked briefly at Anne Mercer. The woman seemed to have literally shrunk before her eyes. She was huddled over her plate, barely touching her food, her blue-white skin unpleasantly pale with tension and misery. She was avoiding looking at anyone, and Hannah noticed with irritated compassion that her hand shook as she lifted a forkful of food to her mouth.

Her husband, who should have been the one to notice these symptoms of his wife's distress, was totally oblivious to her. He had reached across the table to squeeze Fiona's hand, and Hannah felt pretty sure that the heavy thigh she had felt pressing exploratively against her own belonged to him, and that its contact had not been intended for her at all. She had retaliated by stabbing the instep of his foot with her high heel, and then apologising sweetly and falsely.

Silas, whom she had thought too engrossed in his conversation with Fiona to notice what was going on, had broken off what he was saying to give her an extremely sharp look which she had returned with rebellious pride.

Now, thank heaven, the meal was almost over. How on earth she was going to endure spending an hour or so closeted with Anne Mercer and Fiona while the men talked business she really had no idea.

When Fiona gave the signal for the ladies to leave, treating Silas to a gurgle of laughter and clinging provocatively to his jacket as she whispered something in his ear, Hannah thought with distaste that this must be the worst dinner party she had endured.

It was, she thought with vehement mental bitterness an hour later: seated opposite Fiona on what had to be the most uncomfortable chair she had ever been invited to occupy, gritting her teeth against the explosion she could feel building up inside her as Fiona alternately toyed with Anne Mercer with all the refined cruelty of a hunting cat, and tried to question Hannah about the exact nature of *her* relationship with Silas. There was a good deal of innuendo in her questions, and an almost open prurience that made Hannah feel physically sick.

She had stated already that she was Silas's personal assistant and that she knew nothing about his personal life and was most certainly not involved in it, but to her astonishment Fiona refused to let the matter rest there.

She had mentioned the fact that Hannah would be spending the night under the same roof as Silas, and had even had the gall to question her about her past and present lovers. Hannah had remained grim-lipped and uninformative, mentally acknowledging that she had wrongly accused Silas on one subject at least. He was obviously not sexually involved with Fiona—at least, not yet—since the other woman was making it plain exactly how she felt about him.

Hannah had been stunned when Fiona had casually mentioned that she believed a marriage benefited from both partners having lovers; she had gone on to say speculatively that she supposed Silas must have many women in his life. Hannah had replied frigidly that she had no idea. Now Fiona, very obviously furious at her refusal to give her any information, was trying a different tack.

'How very businesslike you are, but you must have noticed how sexy Silas is,' she prodded, her smile wide, but her eyes cold and watchful.

'Not really,' Hannah fibbed.

The coldness increased, the mouth hardening a fraction.

'Don't tell me you're one of those women who isn't interested in men,' she asked unforgivably.

Hannah gave her a withering look and said quietly, 'It depends in what context. Certainly I have no desire to marry, if that's what you mean, but neither am I sexually interested in my own sex.'

Behind her she heard Anne Mercer give a tiny shocked gasp, and she smiled thinly. She would die before she gave Fiona the opening she knew she was looking for. One hint to the other woman of her feelings for Silas, and Fiona would use them to destroy and humiliate her. She had no illusions about the older woman, none at all, and it was with a feeling of tremendous relief that she heard the door open and saw that the men had at long last come to join them.

At last it was time to leave. She stood up with a speed that wasn't missed by either Silas or Fiona.

'There's really no need for you to rush off, Silas. Stay and have another couple of drinks. We can always put you up if you're worried about driving. In separate rooms, of course!' She gave a throaty, affected laugh. 'I can't understand how Hannah is managing to remain immune to you, Silas, but apparently she is. She assures me that you're the very last man she would be likely to find attractive.'

Hannah felt her face burn as Silas turned to look at her. What must he be thinking? She hated the way Fiona was reducing her to her own level, interested in nothing more than the appeasement of her own shallow emotions and greedy desires, and yet stupidly when Silas returned in an even voice, 'Hannah is my personal assistant, a business colleague,' she didn't feel in the least mollified. Quite the opposite, in fact.

As Lord Redvers escorted them to the door, Hannah saw Anne Mercer give one despairing, longing look after them. What a silly woman! It was time she stood up to her husband, who was behaving more like a spoilt, bullying child than an adult.

She said as much to Silas as they reached the car, the emotions inside her too explosive to be controlled.

In the light from the windows she saw the cool, considering look he gave her, and winced inwardly, furious with herself for betraying so much emotion.

'I agree; but she obviously loves him, which makes it hard for her.'

'A handicap carried by far too many women,' Hannah said bitterly, 'and exploited by far too many men.'

He unlocked the car and she got in, waiting until he was seated beside her and starting the engine before saying explosively, 'I detest men like that.'

'And women like Fiona?' Silas asked her drily.

She looked at him, and then decided to throw tact to the winds.

'The very worst of our sex,' she said baldly. 'Avaricious, sexually and materially . . . cruel, shallow . . . vindictive.'

'I agree,' Silas said promptly, silencing her. 'But unfortunately Lord Redvers dotes on her, and I've come too far with this project to risk it now by getting on the wrong side of her.'

'Was that why you let her paw you all through dinner?' Hannah challenged acidly, and then realised what she was saying and to whom. Her face went scarlet, and her fingers curled into hard fists. Without removing his attention from the road, Silas picked up her right hand, his stronger fingers prising hers open. She could hear the warmth in his voice as he apologised, 'I'm sorry. I can see she's been giving you a difficult time.'

'She seemed to find it hard to accept that you and I are merely business associates,' Hannah excused her tension weakly. To her chagrin her voice trembled, just as her body was starting to tremble. A physical reaction to her release from her earlier tension, she tried to tell herself, but she knew it wasn't true. It was *Silas* who was having this effect on her. *Silas* who was making her shake with physical and emotional yearning for him. *Silas* who had the power to move her to hitherto unknown depths of feeling simply by speaking to her. By looking at her . . . by touching her as he was doing now. If he could make her feel like this just by stroking her fingers, what would she feel if . . .?

He was still holding her hand.

'Did she? I wonder why.'

Something about the way he said the words made her body shake. Fear and anger mingled inside her, rushing through her. What was Silas trying to imply? That he realised she was attracted to him?

Oh, please, no. She wanted neither his pity nor his participation. Unlike other women in her situation, she had no desire for him to turn to her and see her as a woman . . . to want her physically and emotionally—to love her.

Everything she had witnessed tonight had only confirmed her deeply held belief that marriage was not for her; she would want too much—total commitment, total sharing. Her parents loved one another very deeply indeed, but how many times had she seen her mother forced to take a back seat to her father's parishioners, to his duties and responsibilities? Her mother seemed to accept it, but she didn't think she could. Perhaps all those years of growing up with so many older brothers had left her with too fierce a desire to have herself acknowledged as the equal of any man, as worthy of time, attention and consideration as him, to enable her to accept second place. And children . . . She had never wanted children, never even thought about wanting them, but when she looked at Silas there was a tiny, curling, weakening sensation there inside her that whispered seductively to her that there would be much joy in having this man's child.

She was appalled that she could even form such a thought, never mind be forced to acknowledge it, so appalled that she sat bolt upright in her seat, and turned her face away from Silas, saying dismissively, 'We all make misjudgements. When I saw Fiona in your car with you the other weekend, I assumed from her demeanour toward you that she was already your mistress. However, what she said to me tonight proved that I made a mistake.'

It was that fateful word 'already' that gave her away. How bitterly she wished she could recall it when she almost felt the searing look Silas gave her as he braked hard and demanded explosively, 'Just what exactly are you trying to say? Lord Redvers is very important to my plans for Padley Court, but at no time have I or shall I become his wife's lover.'

She should have left it there, but she couldn't, unable to stop herself from saying acidly, 'Do you think that Fiona will accept that? She struck me as a very determined woman. She told me openly that she believes affairs outside a marriage strengthen it, and she made it equally clear how she feels about you. If she has as much influence with her husband as you say, isn't it feasible that she could destroy everything that you've worked for if you turn her down?'

For a moment Hannah genuinely thought she had gone too far. She was prying into an area of Silas's life that had nothing to do with her, betrayed by her genuine curiosity about how he might deal with such a situation into asking questions which would better have remained unvoiced.

He was silent for a long time, so long that she thought he meant to ignore her questions, and then at last he said quietly, 'I can't deny that what you say is true. However, I believe I can make it plain . . . indeed, I *have* made it plain to Fiona, without actually having to reject her, that we aren't going to have an affair. If she refused to accept the situation, then I shall try to arrange all my future meetings with Lord Redvers not to include her.'

'Wouldn't it be simpler and more honest to just tell her the truth?' Hannah asked him cynically.

She felt him looking at her. 'Is that how you deal with unwanted advances, Hannah? Bluntly and efficiently?'

'Women aren't in the same situation as men,' she reminded him bitterly. 'If we don't give an unequivocal "no" we are accused of teasing, of saying "no" when we mean "yes". I prefer to make my position perfectly clear. In the long run, it's more honest and more sensible.'

She noticed that they were almost back at the Dower House; her nerves felt as tightly strung as tension wire. She knew it would be hours before she got to sleep, if indeed she managed to sleep at all.

'So you don't feel that for the sake of the single parents and children who hopefully will one day benefit from our plans for the place, I should put aside my personal feelings and beliefs and—er—give in to Fiona's blandishments?'

The implications of his questions, coming so unexpectedly out of the darkness, flooded her mind and body with dark, unfamiliar pain. It came at her like a tidal wave, destructive and dangerous, crashing down through the barriers of her defences, swirling icily through the most private corners of her being, opening her to anguish and reality so that she had to grit her teeth together to stop herself from giving vent to what she was feeling, to buy herself time.

'No answer? It's a tricky one, isn't it?' he said quietly.

He had turned off the main road now, and the entrance to the drive loomed ahead of them. He turned into it, and in the car's headlights she saw the familiar bulk of the house. How many thousands of children would this house give pleasure to if Silas's plans were successful? The greater good . . . the words beat drearily through her, almost like a dirge.

The car swept round the drive towards the Dower House. Silas switched off the engine.

'If I were to ask you, what would you advise me to do, I wonder? Fiona is a creature of greedy impulse, soon satiated and bored. A few nights together . . . the basic mechanics of making love . . .'

Hannah felt her gorge rise. Unable to stop herself, she pushed open the car door and started to run towards the house. She couldn't listen to any more without betraying something of what she was going through. The mere thought of him with Fiona in his arms, of that greedy, predatory mouth on his . . .

He caught her half-way towards the door, spinning her round with such force that she staggered and almost lost her balance.

As he held on to her, he asked grimly, 'What the hell was that for?'

The easy mood of insouciant sophistication was gone. Her stomach trembled as she looked into his face and saw the tamped down maleness there, the essential predatory masculinity . . .

'Nothing,' she lied. 'I don't care what you do.

Go and make love to Fiona, if that's what you want.'

'But it isn't what I want.'

How silky his voice sounded, seducing her senses away from her.

'*She* isn't what I want. Ironic, isn't it? All evening, while I've been struggling to hold *her* at bay, I've been wondering what it would be like to hold *you* like this . . .'

He had shifted his weight somehow so that she was almost leaning full length against him, her breasts pressed hard and flat against his chest, her body encircled by his arm so that she couldn't move away. Her thighs against his, the sudden, heart-stopping movement of his free hand along the contour of her hip up over her waist to rest just beneath the fullness of her breasts, made the breath lock in her throat and her body tremble with awareness of his own arousal.

'Hannah . . .' He said her name as though he was tasting it. His mouth touched her jaw and moved over her skin tantalisingly, drawing closer and closer to her lips.

She could feel herself quivering with an anticipation she made no attempt to fight or hide.

When his mouth finally touched hers, she wasn't sure which of them gave that tiny, betraying sigh of satisfaction, but there was no mistaking the way her body melted into his embrace, the way her breast swelled into his hand, so that he made a husky sound of pleasure deep in his throat and stroked his tongue over her lips, over and over again until the torment of that delicate touch made her cry out softly and tremble, blind to everything but the satisfaction of at least feeling his mouth moving so savagely and eagerly against her own.

She responded to the passion she could sense inside him in full measure, allowing him the access he sought to her body as he moved her within his arms and cursed against her lips at the dress that prevented his lean fingers from doing anything more than merely shaping the round swell of her breasts.

The arousal of his body, her own need, the fierce, tumultuous pleasure of feeling him kiss her with all the intimacy and desire she knew she had craved, for a time obliterated everything else.

But only for a time. As he reached behind her for her zip, sanity crashed through her sensual haze; released from the confinement of his arms, she sprang back from him, panic and self-disgust written plainly on her face for him to see.

Almost loathing herself for her own self-betrayal, she made no attempt to hide her reactions, and Silas, seeing them, said quietly, 'I'm sorry. I shouldn't have done that.'

'No, you shouldn't,' Hannah agreed shakily, conveniently forgetting how very little discouragement she had given him. And, also forgetting what he'd said before kissing her, she added unforgivably, 'I'm not Fiona. There's nothing to be gained from making love to me.'

There was a long silence, during which she found that she couldn't meet his eyes; she felt almost ashamed . . . and not just ashamed, but hurt inside, as though she wanted him to deny what she was saying and take her back in his arms. Instead he said quietly, so quietly that she barely heard him, 'No. It doesn't seem as though there is.'

And then, without another word, he walked past her and unlocked the door to the house, holding it open and waiting politely and distantly until she followed him inside.

CHAPTER NINE

AS SHE had already mentally predicted, Hannah got very little sleep. A whole night spent virtually wide awake, with no distraction other than that caused by the ancient grumblings of an old house, was a marvellous way of focusing the mind, Hannah reflected while she dressed.

Although she had tussled with the problem virtually all night, she had known from the outset that there was only once course she could take.

She would have to resign from her job with Silas. Not specifically because he had kissed her, but because of the way she herself had felt.

The most feminine and secret part of her had recognised in his arms an awareness of herself as a desirable woman, which, if allowed to develop, would lead to all manner of problems; not least the fact that, should Silas choose to lay siege to her sexually, she doubted her ability to reject him.

And so she had no alternative. The moment they were back in London she intended to hand him her written resignation. It was better that way, allowing no room for arguments. She ignored the tiny voice that mocked her for being a coward, telling her that she lacked the courage to meet him face to face in the intimacy of his home, and tell him what she planned to do.

What her emotional female inner self termed cowardice, her outer, more rational mind deemed mere caution and common sense. There was no point in deliberately courting danger, in almost actively inviting the very kind of explosive situation she was fighting to avoid.

She tried to imagine what might have happened last night had Silas not stepped back from her when he did . . . had she been wearing something that had allowed him easier access to her body . . . had she felt his hands against her skin, while his mouth was still on hers, obliterating all rationality.

She wouldn't have been able to resist the deep-rooted urge of her own nature, the need she had so desperately fought against ever since they had met. She would have willingly urged him to take her upstairs to the privacy of his bedroom, to strip the clothes from her body and make love to her. She shivered in the morning chill, staring blindly out of her bedroom window and across the mist-enshrouded landscape.

Beyond the mist, in the far distance, the sun was starting to break through the cloud. The storm was over, just like the storm within her. She shivered again, acknowledging that hand in hand with her belief that she had made the right, indeed the only decision, went a bleak awareness of all that she was turning her back on.

Fiona hadn't lied or exaggerated when she had claimed that Silas would be a lover that few women could resist. Last night Hannah had experienced the full magnetic force of his sensuality. She had felt instinctively, intuitively, that he was one of those rare men who genuinely believed womankind to be his equal, and at the same time retained an essential maleness that allowed him to accept such knowledge with grace and still to treat her sex with tenderness and caring.

He was a man wholly proud and at ease with his masculinity, and yet who appreciated everything that was different about a woman.

Even now, with her decision made and irreversible, there was still a part of her that yearned most dangerously to turn back the clock and relive last night, but to give it a different ending . . . one that allowed her to spend the night in Silas's arms, to wake up basking in the warmth of his desire. But she had to quell that weakness, to destroy it, to submerge it in other and more sensible thoughts.

It was time to go down for breakfast.

Silas was already seated at the table. He stood up as she walked in, and gave her a cool, assessing glance, which she withstood with as much calm as she could, proffering a professional, distancing smile as she sat down in the chair he pulled out for her, commenting brightly on the change in the weather, asking what time he planned to return to London.

'Like you, I feel that I might as well stay on and enjoy the benefits of a weekend in the country. We should have got through the rest of the work here by mid-afternoon. I'll run you over to your parents then, and we can arrange what time I'll pick you up on Monday morning.'

Beneath her immaculate silk shirt and thick tweed sweater, Hannah felt her heart start to pound rapidly.

'That won't be necessary,' she told him, softening the baldness of the words with a brief smile. 'It will be quite easy for me to get the train to London. There's no point in you coming out of your way.'

She saw the way his whole face darkened, and sensed the anger he was fighting to control, acknowledging with an inward shiver that he could be extremely intimidating.

'As far as I am aware, your parents' village isn't out of my way,' he told her frigidly. 'However, if you prefer to make your own arrangements . . .'

'I . . . I thought I might go back to London early on Sunday. There are one or two things I want to do. People I need to see . . .'

His eyebrows lifted, an expression of cynicism twisting his mouth as he said silkily, 'There's no need to be afraid of speaking bluntly to me, Hannah. If you mean that you want to return to London because you wish to be with a man—a lover—then by all means say so.'

'If I did, I would,' Hannah interrupted him hotly, forgetting her danger and the need for self-preservation in her need to deny his cynicism. 'Your implication was unwarranted, especially when you already know that I'm not involved in that kind of relationship. Nor do I want to be.'

She saw a faint shadow touch his eyes, and wondered what she had said to cause it. His mouth became grim, his voice unusually harsh as he said curtly, 'I'm sorry. Your private time and how you spend it is, of course, your own concern. If you wish to make your own arrangements to travel back to London, then naturally you must do so. Now, I suggest that we make an early start on the work we need to get through.

'I'm going to make a call to London to find out if there's anything there that needs my attention. If you could be in my study at ten o'clock, we can talk about the responsibilities I want you to take on personally with regard to the redevelopment of the Court.'

As he got up and pushed back his chair, Hannah reflected guiltily that she really ought to tell him now that she intended to hand in her notice. It wasn't fair to allow him to waste his time involving her in what was patently a project very close to his heart, when she knew she was not going to be working on it.

But she *couldn't* tell him. Not now, not here. And she didn't want to go too deeply into her own reasons for not wanting to, even though she knew that that reluctance damned her even more firmly.

At ten o'clock she presented herself in the study, and even though Silas worked her hard, displaying the shrewdness and acumen she had heard so much about, even though she was concentrating almost fully on what he was saying to her, a tiny part of her consciousness remained apart to notice how his woollen shirt revealed the muscles of his chest and arms . . . how the jeans he was wearing clung to the leanness of his hips and thighs, how when he got up from behind his desk and paced the floor between it and the window he moved lithely and efficiently, making the blood run hot in her veins . . . When he picked up a book from the window-seat and absently ran his fingers along the leather spine, she shivered inwardly, as though it was her body he had touched. Her mouth went suddenly dry, her lips parting on a slight sound of arousal, which he nevertheless seemed to hear because he turned round abruptly and looked at her, his attention focusing on her mouth so that her heart went crazy, and the sound of its frantic pounding was like the crashing of storm-driven waves against the rocks of some inhospitable coastline.

He had stopped talking. She knew her breathing had become provocatively shallow and, even though she fought to stop herself from doing it, she couldn't prevent her tongue from snaking out and wetting her dry lips.

A shiver seemed to run through him, convulsing his body, making a small muscle twitch in his jaw, and his chest lift deeply, as though he couldn't get enough air to breathe. He lifted his glance from her mouth to her eyes, and his were brilliant with desire and fierce maleness. One tiny step towards him, that was all it would take to release the sexual tension she could almost feel emanating from him. One tiny step and he would be hers . . . He would be reaching for her, enfolding her in his arms, kissing her with all the fierce ruthlessness she could see glittering in his eyes. One tiny step and her body would know the infinitely seductive sensation of his hands upon it. Her breasts, still aching with the need he had aroused in them last night, would know the caressing touch of his fingers, the hot suckle of his mouth. One tiny step . . .

One tiny step and everything she had planned for her life would be lost to her. With an immense effort she managed to break free of the spell of her own sensuality. Dragging her bemused gaze away from him, she said shakily, 'You were saying about the number of single-parent families you hope to offer holidays to at one time . . .'

And although it took him several seconds to follow her lead, several seconds during which she dared not look at him, eventually he did so . . . his voice, when he responded to her prompting, raw with arousal and a dark hint of anger; his body, when eventually she found the courage to look at him, tense with bunched muscles and the kind of self-control that made her throat ache.

When he suggested they work through instead of stopping for lunch so that they could finish work mid-afternoon, she didn't demur. The sooner this appalling day was over, the better. The sooner she could put a much-needed physical distance between them, the better.

She didn't believe she had the strength to hold out against her own need, if she was condemned to spend another twenty-four hours enduring the kind of intimacy she had endured today.

Was it just because she was so aware of him, because she desired him, that she was so intensely aware of every inflexion of his voice, every subtle movement of his body? Or was he *deliberately* tormenting her, making her aware of his masculinity, making her focus on him as a man, as he paced the room, as he almost forced her by some power she could only guess at to focus almost completely on him?

It was three o'clock before he had finished briefing her.

'How long will it take you to get ready to leave?' he asked her curtly, glancing at his own watch.

'Half an hour at the most,' Hannah responded, equally coolly.

'Right, I'll meet you down here at half-past three, then.'

He let her get as far as the door, and then said quietly, 'Hannah . . . about last night . . .'

She held her breath, feeling as though her lungs were being squeezed by an unknown force. She couldn't turn round and look at him, even though she knew she should.

Frantically she wondered what on earth she was supposed to say, and then opted for what she hoped was the safest course, deliberately misunderstanding and saying coolly, 'I hope I haven't prejudiced your plans by reacting so badly to Lady Redvers.'

And then, before he could stop her she was through the door, although she thought she heard him swear, just as she closed it, 'To hell with bloody Fiona!'

Hannah would have given anything to be able to drive herself to her parents, but since she had no form of transport, and since to insist on calling a taxi would have been ridiculous, she was forced to endure the almost stifling intimacy of Silas's presence and Silas's car and Silas's silence as he drove towards her home village.

The journey, which should have been pleasantly relaxing, for the roads were relatively free of traffic and the afternoon was balmy and fine, was instead a refined form of torture.

When she saw the familiar church spire in the distance, Hannah almost heaved a sigh of relief, shakily giving Silas directions as they approached the village.

Instead of stopping outside the house as she had hoped, he turned into the drive and, as ill-luck would have it, her mother was kneeling beside one of the borders, busily weeding.

Of course, Hannah was obliged to introduce her to Silas, and after she had laughingly said how pleased she and Hannah's father were about her new job, because they had benefited through being given Hannah's virtually brand new car, she insisted on offering Silas a cup of tea and something to eat.

Expecting him to refuse, Hannah's heart sank when he accepted and seemed genuinely pleased to allow her mother to lead the way to the back door, pausing every now and again to compliment her on the garden, talking so knowledgeably about it that Hannah was surprised into numb silence.

As always on a Friday afternoon, her father was in his study putting the finishing touches to his sermon, but he appeared from this private retreat to be introduced to Silas, and when the four of them sat down to the generous afternoon tea her mother had provided Hannah discovered that *she* was the one who remained silent, while Silas and her parents talked with the ease and familiarity of very old friends.

It was well over an hour before he got up to leave, during which time Hannah had grown steadily more tense.

When she walked out to his car with him, she felt totally unable to speak, even when she saw the coldly impatient look he gave her and the hard compression of his mouth. As he got into his car, his manner towards her was coolly distant, mimicking her own towards him. It was what she wanted, and yet, oh, how it hurt.

As he switched on the engine, she ached to lean forwards and touch her fingers to his mouth, stroking away its cynical twist, but such dangerous thoughts only reinforced her awareness of how dangerously vulnerable she had become.

As he drove away, she turned her back on him and headed back to the house, only to stop after half a dozen paces, unable to give up the hurting pleasure of turning round to watch him until he was out of sight.

'What a charming man,' her mother commented predictably when she rejoined her parents.

Less predictably, her father remarked in that vague manner of his that at times had driven his offspring mad, but which with maturity they all recognised as springing from his genuine absorption with his pastoral responsibilities, 'I liked him; a thoroughly intelligent and well-informed man. You must find working with him an enjoyable challenge.'

Hannah ducked her head. She was beginning to realise how difficult it was going to be to explain to her parents, but more especially to her mother, just why she had resigned from her prestigious job. She even wondered for a craven heartbeat of time if she could possibly pretend that Silas had sacked her, but then dismissed this fiction as unworthy both of herself and him.

She was gnawing worriedly at her bottom lip, her eyes clouded with emotions, when her mother walked into the room and asked quietly, 'What's wrong?'

She had forgotten her mother's almost diabolic percipience, Hannah acknowledged ruefully, too startled to conceal her expression. She knew that she was guilty of discriminating against her own sex, of making the classic mistake of believing that because a woman chose not to have a career that it necessarily meant that she was lacking in intelligence.

In fact she knew quite well that her parents had met while both were up at Oxford, and that her mother had apparently willingly given up the challenge of a potentially promising career to marry her father.

Now, looking into her mother's concerned face, she felt ashamed and vaguely disquieted. What was it about her that made her selfishly cling so single-mindedly to her determination to remain free of any emotional commitment? Certainly not the example set her by her parents. Without being aware that she intended to do so, she heard herself saying shakily, 'I'm going to resign from my job on Monday.'

Aghast, she waited for her mother's cries of astonishment and shock, but instead, and even more shocking, her mother said quietly, 'Because you've fallen in love with Silas . . .'

For a moment Hannah felt as though her heart was going to stop beating. Then it started to pound with sledgehammer blows that shook her entire body, and she stared at her mother, her colour draining so quickly that the former stretched out a comforting hand to touch her arm and said gently, 'Don't worry. I doubt that anyone else has noticed.' And then, with a small half-smile, she added wryly, 'After all, I *am* your mother, and despite the fact that all of you appear to think of me as a creature completely lacking in intelligence at times, I know all of you so well that it's easy for me to judge your feelings.'

Mingled with her shock was a fine thread of guilt and regret for the truth her mother had spoken so wryly, but she wasn't given any opportunity to dwell on it because her mother sat down next to her and asked calmly, 'What is it that worries you so much, Hannah? A fear that Silas doesn't return your feelings, or a fear that he does?'

The calm words affected her like an electric shock, making her head jerk up and her eyes widen with disbelief. 'How did you know? How did you know I felt like that?' she asked helplessly.

Her mother smiled.

'Hannah, ever since you were a little girl you've avoided emotional commitment. I've always blamed myself. All those brothers . . . so rough and sometimes unkind to a little girl . . . so competitive, despite all that your father and I tried to do to moderate that instinct.

'There's nothing weak about loving someone, you

know, Hannah. On the contrary, to truly love another human being requires enormous reserves of strength, courage, belief . . .'

Listening to her, Hannah gave a deep shudder and said rawly, 'But I don't *want* to love him. I don't *want* that kind of dependence, that degree of need.' She turned to her mother and said bitterly, 'Modern relationships are such fragile things. Marriages break up every day; people hurt one another, and always it seems to me that someone within that relationship is hurt so badly that they never recover.

'That terrifies me, Mother. You see, I know instinctively that once I allowed myself to love someone, once I'd made that commitment . . . if the relationship ever broke down, it would destroy me . . .'

It was only as she heard the echoes of her own voice dying away in the stillness of the room that Hannah recognised the emotion in it, the plea she cried out. Half ashamed of her own uninhibitedness, she added gruffly, 'And then there's my career. I *want* to work. I *need* to work.'

Well, there's no reason why you shouldn't,' her mother announced calmly, much to Hannah's astonishment. 'It's my belief that a contented, fulfilled woman makes a better wife and mother than one who feels that her personality is being stifled, who feels resentful of the claims of her husband and children. Hannah,' she took hold of her daughter's hand, turning it over so that she could study her smooth palm, 'Hannah, a man who loves you would understand that need you've just expressed. He wouldn't try to make you conform to a pattern you couldn't fit.'

'Would Dad have allowed you to work if you'd wanted to?' Hannah asked wryly.

Her mother's laughter confounded her.

'My dear, even my generation would take exception to being ''allowed'' to do anything by their husbands. Had I wanted a career outside that of being a vicar's wife, had he seen how important that career was to me, I know your father would have tried his best to accommodate my need. *That's* what a good relationship is all about, Hannah . . . trying to accommodate one another's needs, making allowances for them, and understanding that when we love someone we must love the whole person, not just specific bits of them.' She released Hannah's hand and got up.

'Believe me, Hannah, I'm not trying to pressure you into anything, but, my dear, I'd hate to see you ruin your whole life simply because you're afraid . . .'

Afraid. How easily her mother had read her, Hannah realised when she was alone. How small and immature her mother had made her feel with her wisdom; how shallow and selfish in her judgements and motives.

She moved restlessly around the room. None of what her mother had said made any difference, though; she was still determined to hand in her notice. She couldn't afford the risks, the potential anguish that loving Silas would bring . . . not so much because she couldn't bear to relinquish her own plans for her life, but because she couldn't endure the thought of loving him, of *being* loved by him . . . only to lose him. There was to be no going back. She had made up her mind, and she intended to stick to her decision to hand in her notice, no matter what emotional anguish that decision brought her.

CHAPTER TEN

IN THE END, Hannah didn't return home to her docklands apartment until late on Sunday evening. She was unwilling to be alone with her own thoughts, desperate to prevent herself from weakening and letting her emotions triumph over her resolution.

The train seemed to stop at every station and to take for ever to reach London, and then there was the lengthy tube journey across the city itself, but at last she was back in her own private place.

Too weary to do anything other than go straight to bed, she showered briefly, and then, before she could weaken completely, she sat down and typed out her resignation.

There was no need to use specifics, and she took refuge in the lie that she felt her skills were incompatible with the job, knowing that Silas wouldn't have any problem at all in finding someone to take her place.

She then went to bed, so exhausted that she fell into a deep sleep almost straight away. But an observer would not have found her sleep untroubled. She moved restlessly from one side of the bed to the other, calling out Silas's name several times in a hopeless, yearning way that reflected her inner feelings, tears she didn't know she cried dampening her face, as though that part of her nature that her waking mind deemed weak and vulnerable was already mourning the death of something special that would never come again.

She was awake early and at the office for eight, relieved to discover that she had arrived before Maggie and Sarah.

She slipped into Silas's office and left her resignation on his desk, knowing that he would see it the moment he walked in, since Maggie never produced the post until fifteen minutes or so after his arrival, and then she went back to her own office and waited in a fret of tension while conscientiously trying to sort out anything of priority on her desk.

She had closed the communicating door between her office and Silas's, but even so she heard the outer door open and knew that he had arrived.

She tried to ignore the small sounds coming from his office, to ignore the tension that built up inside her with every passing second, not to visualise what he was doing, how he would look when he found her letter and read it, not to look fearfully at the closed communicating door.

When her intercom bleeped, she stared numbly at it, reluctantly depressing the answer key.

'Hannah, come in here, will you?'

No 'please'. No question of his order—because order it was—being refused.

Hannah got up on shaky legs, trying to master her apprehension as she walked towards the communicating door and opened it.

Silas was seated behind his desk. He looked up at her with a frown as she walked towards him. Her letter lay opened on his desk.

'Sit down,' he told her grimly.

Weakly she did so, her heart quailing as he got up and walked around the desk towards her, perching on the edge of it, not perhaps deliberately intimidating her, but the effect was there, none the less. It *was* intimidating having him so close to her that the scent of his body, mingling with the soap and cologne he used, should torment her own senses into flaring awareness of him . . . not as her boss, but as a man.

'What exactly is the meaning of this?' he demanded silkily, holding her letter.

Hannah couldn't look at him. Instead she focused on the window behind his desk, as she said as steadily as she could, 'I thought my letter was self-explanatory. I'm handing in my resignation.'

'Because you find your skills are not compatible with the responsibility of the job,' he taunted her bitingly, reading from her letter. 'Come on, Hannah. You know that's nonsense. If that had been the case, you'd never been offered the job in the first place. What's going on? Or can I guess?' he suggested softly.

So softly that she was trapped into looking directly at him, and then wished she hadn't as she found herself mesmerised by the silky challenge of his gaze.

'You want to leave because of what happened between us the other night, don't you?' he challenged.

Hannah swallowed. Her voice seemed to have become trapped somewhere in her throat. She shook her head, and then said explosively, her voice raw and husky, 'I don't want to discuss it.'

'No, I can see that. For pity's sake, Hannah, you're

a sophisticated, educated woman. What was it about one kiss that makes you turn your back on a job we both *know* you're ideally suited for? If it bothered you so much . . .'

'It didn't,' Hannah lied desperately, stepping back from him, suddenly so desperately aware of him, so conscious of her danger, so terrified of what she might betray if she stayed and let him continue to question her that she fled to the door before he could stop her, saying huskily as she reached it, 'I'm leaving, Silas. That's all I need to tell you.'

'Hannah!'

She froze as he bellowed her name, knowing that he was going to come after her, and then to her relief Gordon Giles, who had returned that morning, walked into the room, smiling genially at her, and saying urgently to Silas, 'Silas, I need to talk to you. Something's come up with the Howland people. Can you spare me ten minutes now?'

Almost tangibly aware of the frustration he was experiencing, Hannah didn't wait to hear what he replied. Instead she went into her own office, checked through the already tidy drawers, picked up her coat, and was half-way towards the lift before she realised that she was safe and that Silas wasn't going to come after her.

She didn't want to go straight home, unwilling to face the silence of her flat, but she knew she had little alternative. She was going to have to start looking for a new job immediately, and she was probably going to have to reclaim her car from her father. She felt guilty about that, but she knew he would understand.

The phone rang a couple of times during the day,

but she was terrified of answering it, just in case it was Silas trying to persuade her to change her mind.

A week passed; the longest week of Hannah's life. Even though she knew there were things she had to do, she felt no sense of urgency, no motivation, no purpose. For the first time since she had left university, her life was not directed towards a specific goal.

For some inexplicable reason, her career, the cornerstone of her life, meant nothing.

Instead of scouring the papers for a new job, instead of approaching the upmarket and discreet agencies which handled the high-powered positions for which she was qualified, she found herself simply sitting and staring into space, watching the river for hour after hour.

Her mother was concerned enough about her to make the trek to London, arriving anxiously and unexpectedly on Friday morning, and insisting on dragging Hannah out to do some shopping when she discovered how little food she had in her fridge.

'Starving yourself isn't going to achieve anything,' she announced forthrightly, causing Hannah to object and then fall silent as she realised how long it actually was since she had last eaten properly.

'Hannah, it isn't too late . . .' her mother said softly once they were back at the apartment and sitting down to the meal she had prepared. 'Get in touch with Silas. Tell him you made a mistake.'

But before she could finish Hannah was shaking her head. 'It's no use,' she said dully. 'If he'd wanted me back, he'd have been in touch with me himself.'

She turned to her mother and said self-contemptuously, 'He probably recognised the way I feel about him. Just as you did. The classic office syndrome . . . falling in love with one's boss.'

While her mouth turned down bitterly with the full painful weight of her own self-analysis, her mother watched her unhappily.

'Hannah, come home,' she suggested impulsively. 'It will do you good . . .'

Hannah gave her a wry smile.

'Crawl back into the safety of the parental nest? You don't know how tempting that is.' She stood up and paced the small room like a caged animal, her body wild with tension and pain, and much as her mother ached to help her she knew there was nothing she could do.

'It's ironic, isn't it?' Hannah said at last, swinging round to look at her. 'The ultimate career woman. That's me. I've done exactly what I know is right, and yet I feel as though my whole life has suddenly blown up in my face. If I come home now, I'll never find the guts to leave again,' she said tiredly. 'I've got to work this out for myself, and the first thing I've got to do is to find another job.'

She spent the entire weekend doing so, only giving in to the exhaustion and misery on Monday evening when she got home from a round of agency interviews, during which she had inexplicably found herself totally uninterested in every position that had been suggested.

Too exhausted to change out of her interview uniform of pin-striped suit and tailored silk shirt, she slumped into a chair and lay there with her eyes closed, trying to summon the will to fight the feeling inside her which grew every day.

Being apart from Silas hadn't killed her love for him. On the contrary, her feelings only seemed to grow sharper and more intense with every day that passed. Instead of being free to concentrate on her career and her life plan, she found herself dwelling almost obsessively on every second of the time she had spent with him, going over and over again every small incident . . . not as she had fully intended, putting her time with him in the past as a closed incident, so that she could go on into her carefully planned future, but totally abandoning that future in favour of minutely reliving every small particle of time she had spent with Silas.

She could barely understand it, or the change in herself, and could only cling grimly to her faltering belief that she had done the right thing.

Common sense urged her to get up and make herself something to eat. She had gone out without breakfast and been out all day without a meal. Her appearance was beginning to suffer for it: her hair and skin becoming lacklustre, her energy levels dropping dramatically.

In the distance she heard her doorbell ring. Reluctantly she opened her eyes. Not her mother again, surely? And yet there was a tiny betraying spark of hope that it might be. A telling weakness that showed her more than anything else how vulnerable she had become. Telling herself that it was probably only one of her neighbours on the cadge, she went to answer the bell's sharp summons.

The evenings were drawing in early now; they were well into autumn, and the coolness of the air as she opened the door made her shiver convulsively, and think longingly of the vicarage's large open log-burning fires, forgetting in the nostalgia of the moment the inconvenience of cleaning them out.

Lost in her own private thoughts, the figure outside the door remained only a shadowy entity in the darkness until he stepped forwards and into her hallway, enunciating fiercely, 'Hannah!' as he saw her shudder in recognition and mistook its cause.

At the sound of his voice, every nerve-ending in her body had become alert.

Silas! Silas, here . . . The joyful leap of her heart, the fierce, pounding, dizzying pleasure that rocked her, told their own story, even though in their aftermath she might feel dread and anger that he had breached her defences and invaded the privacy of her home.

She shivered again, her teeth chattering, and this time he realised it wasn't revulsion at the sight of him that caused her tremors. Seizing her arm, he slammed the door and bundled her towards her sitting-room, wincing a little in the harshness of the overhead lights, and glaring belligerently around the starkly furnished room as he muttered, 'Haven't you heard of subdued lighting?'

Almost as though it was someone else who spoke the words, Hannah heard herself saying quietly, 'Subdued lighting is for lovers. I don't need it.'

Her emotionless words seemed to set off some kind of explosion in Silas, as he thrust her down into her sofa. He stood towering over her and enunciated bitterly, 'Just as you don't need me, is that it, Hannah? You've made quite a career out of not needing things—and people—haven't you? Of standing alone, of doing your own thing and to hell with anyone else . . .'

Hannah felt her face burn; there was just enough truth in his accusation to make her feel uncomfortable, but she tried to defend herself by saying quickly, 'It's my affair how I choose to live my life!' And then she got up and put as much distance between them as she could, standing defensively with her back to him as she stared out of the window at the Thames so that she wouldn't have to look at him.

'I don't know why you've come here, Silas.'

'Oh, for pity's sake!' he exploded, and even without looking at him she could feel his anger and winced beneath the force of it. 'Let's forget the obligatory opening passages, shall we, Hannah? They aren't true, anyway. You know damn well why I've come here. The same reason I kissed you, the same reason you gave in your notice, the same reason you haven't got the guts to turn round and look at me now, damn you . . .'

And, without her knowing that he had moved, he was suddenly behind her, turning her round, holding her with such fierce urgency that her blood started to beat a wild tattoo of delirium through her veins, despite her attempts to stop it.

'I've tried not to do this,' she heard him saying in an unfamiliar, thickened voice, while his mouth was buried in the warmth of her throat, caressing the softness of her skin, making her tremble and turn weak in his arms.

'I've tried to listen to all the logical arguments I've had with myself about the potential impermanence of love, about the problems of sharing my life with a woman who's as goal-orientated as I am myself, about the difficulties we'll face, but none of it makes the slightest damn difference. I close my eyes, and I can see you and feel you, and my body dissolves in the kind of heat I haven't felt in ten years, if then; and all I want to do is to hold you like this . . . to touch you . . . to kiss you . . .'

His voice faded—muffled by her hair—as his mouth caressed the silky skin behind her ear, making her quiver, sending startlingly powerful darts of sensation racing through her body.

His teeth nipped her earlobe, his breath warm and moist against it, causing her to draw a deep breath and cling desperately to her rapidly disappearing self-control. As his hand slid inside her jacket and unerringly found and moulded her breast, she reached out to him with agitated hands, pushing firmly against his collarbone with the heel of her palms, while demanding unsteadily, 'Silas, are you mad? How dare you come in here and . . .'

'And what?' he asked her, his mouth so close to her own that she hardly dared to breathe. 'And do this? Or this? But I do dare, Hannah, because I know it's the only way I have of breaking through those defences of yours, of proving to you that you and I can have something worthwhile together.'

She opened her mouth to protest, and found the words silenced as he kissed her. Not tentatively or questioningly, but as though they were already known to one another, as though he was already familiar with her needs and pleasures; as though the mere feel of the moistness of her lips beneath his own was enough to send him out of his mind.

Indeed, he devoured them as though it was, stroking, biting, sucking on their soft outline until Hannah couldn't resist him any longer, and opened her mouth to him with an eagerness she would once have scorned.

His hand tightened against her breast, and he made a thick sound of pleasure in his throat, his fingers tugging at the buttons on her shirt until he had them unfastened and could slide his hand inside it and push aside the barrier of her bra to caress her bare skin.

It was everything she had known it would be, and yet like nothing she had ever dreamed she could feel; she felt both angry and elated that she had not experienced it before, as she felt the sensations roll over her, experiencing them with the same intensity she had once given to her studies—so sharply alive, so intensely aware, so swamped by feeling that she actually felt tears of sharp pleasure spurt in her eyes as his fingers found her nipple.

As her tears touched his mouth, Silas lifted his head and stared into her eyes before she could conceal the expression in them from him, and then said unsteadily, 'Your first time . . . the first time anyone's touched you like this . . . shown you you can feel like this . . . Oh, Hannah, have you any idea what you're doing to me?'

And then it seemed to Hannah that he went a little wild, picking her up with an ease that in other circumstances would have surprised her, but which now seemed wholly natural, carrying her to the sofa, where he nestled her against its cover and proceeded to cover her face with small kisses, and then her throat, so that she arched beneath the heat on his mouth in trembling awareness of her feminity. Then he moved to the open V-neckline of her shirt, and then lower, until his mouth teased the hard peak of her nipple through the silk of her shirt, until she cried out at the unbearable torment, held his hand in her palms and tried to push him away so that she could remove the barrier between them and feel the exquisite sensuality of his mouth tugging at the swollen heat of her nipple. But as she looked down towards him, she saw how the wet silk clung to her body, revealing the pale flesh of her breast and the dark, tormented hardness of its aureole. Silas was breathing heavily, his weight pressing her into the sofa, his body, she now recognised, fully aroused. Her heart missed a beat, and then another. She took a deep breath and shuddered as she felt the drag of the damp fabric against her breast. Her eyes wide and dark with arousal, she removed her hands from his face and down to her blouse. He didn't break the mesmeric hold of his eyes on her own by so much as a flicker of an eyelid, but his face suddenly went dark under a hot rush of blood, and he said thickly, with an urgency that fired her own senses, 'Yes, Hannah . . . Yes . . .'

And, with a deliberate wantonness she had never suspected she might be capable of, never mind actually enjoy, she sat up smoothly, and slowly removed her shirt and then her bra.

No man had ever seen her naked, and she had never desired, nor imagined, that any man would. What she was doing went totally against everything she had planned for her life, and yet, while part of her mind registered the fact, another part gloried in her feminine triumph, telling her to be proud of the beauty of her body and the power it had to make Silas suddenly start to shake and reach for her, burying his face against her throat and groaning as he gently kissed the soft hollow at its base.

'I knew you could be like this, the first time I saw you,' he whispered rawly. 'I wanted you to be like this then, and yet I didn't. I was terrified of the intensity of my reaction to you. You weren't what I wanted in my life. I wasn't ready for a woman like you. In fact, I'd already decided that my life was better off without love. Far less complicated. I felt I owed it to my aunt to concentrate on the business. And then I saw you and it seemed that fate was mocking me.'

Her hand touched his head, stroking the clean, dark hair, a tremor of understanding and compassion rocking through her. All he was doing was echoing her own thoughts. How much less complicated they seemed when they were shared with someone else. How much less important everything seemed when she held him like this and felt the easy warmth of his breath against her skin.

He raised his head abruptly and cupped her face in his hands.

'Hannah, if I stay, I'll make love to you. There's no way I'll be able to stop myself. For over a week I've kept away, telling myself that you don't want me, that your decision was the right one, and then this morning when I woke up I knew I just couldn't go on any longer without you.' He leaned his forehead against hers.

'I don't want you just for today, Hannah. I don't want an affair . . . a relationship without commitment or promises. I may not have wanted to admit it at first, but I love you, so think carefully now, because unless you can open your life to me completely . . . unless you can make enough space in it for me on a permanent basis, it's better that we part now.'

Hannah stared at him. How could he do this to her, torment her like this, while her body ached for him? She didn't want to talk . . . She wanted . . .

She flushed darkly as she realised exactly what she did want. Silas was only being sensible, and it wasn't his fault that half of her wished that he wouldn't be, that he would simply take her and make love to her.

The primitiveness of her own thoughts shocked her. What had happened to her beliefs?

'What is it to be, Hannah?' Silas pressed her. 'A shared life, with all the pain and pleasures that implies? We can work together, side by side, but inevitably there could be times when your career will take second place. I'd be lying if I pretended not to know how much it means to you, and I'd also be lying if I said that I didn't want children.'

Children. Her heart leapt, something raw and elemental twisting inside her. Her hand touched her stomach, almost as though she could already feel Silas's child growing there.

'I want you as my true partner in life, Hannah. As my wife . . . in my business . . . with our children.

I've spoken to your mother,' he added quietly. 'I went to see her, hoping that you might have gone home. She told me how you feel about marriage . . . about your career. We both know that I could make love to you now, and for a space of time nothing would be more important than the private world we can create together, but we can't inhabit that world for the rest of our lives. The decision must be yours, Hannah.'

She wanted to protest that what he was doing wasn't fair. That *she* didn't want the burden of making such a decision, especially not in her present weakened state. Marriage and a career . . . Silas and his children . . . To work with him as his wife and as his partner . . . She had seen the strains those kind of claims put on her sex, and now for the first time she could see why they endured them, why they willingly took on the double burden of marriage and a career, why they claimed that despite the hardships and the sacrifices they still considered themselves doubly blessed and fulfilled.

Without Silas, her life would be hollow and empty. With him, it would be fraught with the inevitable tensions of living and working together . . . of two highly intelligent people, each with their own and sometimes opposing views . . . of juggling different roles and needs.

For the first time since she could remember, the thought of living her life alone held no appeal. Tears stung her eyes as she reflected how often she had seen her mother reach out and touch her father, or vice versa. How often she had witnessed tenderness and caring between couples and deliberately turned her back on it, not wanting to see it.

It wouldn't be easy, but then nothing worth having ever was. If she denied him, turned him away, it would be impossible to wipe him out of her life as though he had never been. She could not simply go on as she had intended, this last week had shown her that.

'Don't be afraid,' he whispered lovingly. 'We can do it together, Hannah.'

Afraid? Suddenly, illuminatingly, she knew that he was right, that she *had* been afraid . . . afraid of giving herself, of committing herself, of sharing herself with another human being, and most of all afraid of failing, of loving and then losing, of pain and loneliness.

She had tasted all of those this last week, and now she was being offered a chance to put them behind her, to reach out and embrace life fully.

She took a deep breath and then said unsteadily and warningly, 'We'll have to be married in my father's church. The whole village will be there and . . .'

'And you'll have roses in your hair,' Silas told her, kissing her fiercely. 'And you'll wear a cream silk dress and not a white one, because no matter what else our lives together hold . . . they're going to hold this night and our memories of it.'

She put her hand over his heart and felt it give a fierce leap, and then he pushed her down into the warmth of the sofa, covering her face and throat and then her breasts with fierce, stinging kisses. Then, when her blood was at delirium heat, his mouth slid over her nipple and she felt the hard pulse of his body against her own.

Her skirt followed his suit on to the floor; her tights and silk briefs joining his discarded socks and shorts.

He let her study him and then touch him until his self-control broke and he started to touch her with his hands and then his mouth, so that there wasn't a centimetre of her silky flesh that he hadn't explored.

When she tried to reciprocate, he wouldn't let her, muttering thickly in her ear, 'Next time . . . It's too late.' And then he moved, taking her with him, spreading the tremulous softness of her thighs, touching her with his body where he had already touched her with his hands and mouth, so that her flesh melted instantly, eagerly anticipating his penetration.

It was unique and special to them alone, and yet at the same time it was the beat of the whole universe, the pulse of its tides, the movements of its planets, the strength of its storms and the spiritual ecstasy of all its gods, so that she felt elevated beyond anything she had ever known; privileged and humbled; knowing that if this one night was the sum total of her life's pleasures then it was more than worthwhile, and equally knowing that it would not be. This sweet, immortal pleasure was something they would have all their lives. She looked drowsily at Silas and saw that he was looking back at her with love and pleasure.

'You didn't mind . . . that there hadn't been anyone else?'

'No . . . and neither would I have minded if there had, just so long as he hadn't been given the rapturous joy you've just given me. I've been lucky.

My previous sexual relationships have all been good—and all ended by mutual agreement—but their pleasure was physical and fleeting. Nothing like this.'

He touched her bare arm while he spoke, running his forefinger along her flesh and laughing softly as the tiny hairs stood on end.

Hannah knew quite well that, against the moist heat of his chest, her breasts were already hardening—and swelling, that inside her body she was already growing soft and moist.

Silas bent his head and lazily licked her skin—like a lion grooming its mate, Hannah thought sensually, abandoning herself to the delicious movement of his tongue as she reached out to caress him in turn.

'It won't always be like this,' Silas warned her seriously. 'There'll be times when you will hate me, when you will resent our lives together.'

'When I'm frightened of the depth of my emotional dependence on you,' Hannah agreed slowly.

'Don't ever be frightened of that. I'm just as dependent on you. When you handed in your notice, I felt as though the bottom had fallen out of my world. I tried to tell myself that I was glad, that your going solved a problem I hadn't wanted to face. I knew damn well there was a mutual danger there, but I hadn't wanted to acknowledge it.

'I fought against what I felt for you, just as you fought against what you feel for me. And I'm glad we both lost.'

'So am I,' Hannah agreed in a heartfelt voice. 'So am I.'

OASIS IS PARADISE...

FOR A PRICE

For the rich, *Oasis* is a fabulous, exclusive world of unlimited luxury.

For the reckless, *Oasis* is a vital clinic – a sanctuary for their drink and drug problems, a hope for their futures.

For the ruthless, *Oasis* is a hotbed of money, power and prestige, which nothing can destroy.

For the reader, *Oasis* is a hot, contemporary novel from top author Patricia Matthews.

Don't miss it!

Published: OCTOBER 1989

WORLDWIDE

Price £3.50

Available from Boots, Martins, John Menzies, W.H. Smith, Woolworths and other paperback stockists.

MAURA SEGER
MAURA SEGER
Elizabeth
MAURA SEGER